The Sheikh's Lost Lover

DESERT KINGS, BOOK 3
Razeen and Lucy

DIANA FRASER

BAY BOOKS

DESERT KINGS

Wanted: A Wife for the Sheikh (1)
The Sheikh's Bargain Bride (2)
The Sheikh's Lost Lover (3)
Awakened by the Sheikh (4)
Claimed by the Sheikh (5)
Wanted: A Baby by the Sheikh (6)

CHAPTER ONE

King Razeen ibn Shad looked across the calm waters of the bay, silvered under the light of the bright moon, and watched his old friend climb aboard the yacht. It had been a good night: dinner and conversation with someone who wasn't his employee or his subject, someone who didn't want anything from him. The shared laughter and memories made the loneliness afterwards even harder to bear. But he had no choice. His country had to come first.

He was about to turn away when a flash of white on the calm waters drew his attention. He narrowed his eyes and saw a swimmer: arms cutting through the sea in a sleek action designed to move fast through water, designed not to disturb the calm surface, designed not to be seen. And it would have worked if he hadn't been watching so closely.

He moved to the shadow of the palm trees that fringed the beach and watched the faint movement on the water come closer. The beach was off-limits until the scientific survey of the coral reef his friend was undertaking was complete. Until then, no one had permission to be here. Last time they'd had intruders, they'd lost part of the coral forever. He'd make sure it didn't happen again.

Lucy stepped out of the sea onto the still-warm sand, squeezed the water out of her long hair and walked up the beach. After a day spent preparing food

below decks, she'd needed a swim—
and what a swim! The water was as
warm as the air that now caressed
her body. She breathed deeply of its
fragrance and looked around.

The beach was a perfect crescent of
white sand under the sheltering sweep
of the palm trees. On one side of the
small bay a rocky promontory jutted
into the water, marking the beginning of
the coral reef the scientists on the boat
were here to study, and on the other
side she could see the uneven outline
of mangrove trees.

She'd traveled all over the world but
nowhere came close to the perfection
of this unspoiled place. The white
sand was almost luminous under the
starlight and three-quarters moon. The
beach was empty: no lights, no people
and no sound but the distant hoot of an
owl and the seductive splash and drag
of the waves. She was quite alone. The
only sign of habitation was a low-lying

mansion in a neighboring bay and the yacht, bobbing lazily out near the reef.

Perfect. Or it would have been if she didn't have to set her plan into action the next day.

She sat down and wriggled her legs against the sand: enjoying the sense of freedom, relishing the sensuous friction of the dry sand against her wet body, willing her mind to forget, for one moment, what her real purpose was in accepting the job that had brought her to Sitra.

Suddenly she stilled and a prickle of alarm ran down her back. She twisted round and scanned the shadows, her ears straining to hear whatever it was that had disturbed her. It took a second scan of the beach before she saw him.

He stepped away from the dark trees, his white shirt and pale trousers glowing softly in the dim light. Icy fear washed through her body as she scrambled to her feet and spun round.

4

"What are *you* doing here? This beach is off-limits." The stranger's deep and powerful voice filled the silence of the night.

She stepped back toward the sea, her body tense, ready to run. She couldn't see his features: his face was in shadow and his dark hair merged with the trees behind him. She couldn't outrun him; he was closer to her than she was to the sea. She took a deep breath, willing herself to calm, forcing herself to think.

"I know it's off limits. So what the hell are you doing here?"

"Answer my question." It was a command from someone used to obedience.

Lucy swallowed the first angry retort that sprang to mind. She was alone with a man much taller and broader than herself. Somehow she didn't think her self-defense moves would have any effect on him. "I'm with the boat over there. The King has employed us to do some work on the reef. I fancied a swim."

"I see." He paused for a moment. "In that case I assume I can trust you not to disturb the coral." His voice had lost its angry tone, but was no less commanding.

She exhaled a breath she hadn't known she was holding. "Yes, of course."

She waited for him to say something further but he didn't. She took another step backwards, suddenly conscious that she was wearing nothing but a flimsy bikini, had no phone, nothing to protect herself, except herself.

"You may stay if you wish."

"No, I was just going." The moon had risen a little higher above the palm trees, casting light on the stranger. He was striking, with a body as powerful as his voice.

"You should come during daylight,

you would appreciate the beauty of the bay better then."

"I'll be working."

"Alex obviously keeps you busy on The Explorer."

"You know him?"

"He's an old friend. I was watching him return to the boat when I saw you." He paused. "It's a shame you won't get a chance to see the beauty of the beach by day. But there are some things here which are better by night. The bay holds secrets."

"I'm here for work, not pleasure." But, just looking at him, "pleasure" was all she could think about.

A slow smile spread across his face as if he could read her thoughts.

"Shame. If you wish, I can show you one of the bay's hidden treasures. It's known only to a few."

"But I don't know you."

"And don't know if you can trust me? Very wise. I am, after all, a stranger to you. However, I'm not a stranger to your captain. We went to University together."

"Which one?"

He smiled. "You are right to be suspicious. We were at Oxford. He studied Marine Biology but makes his money with the family firm—banking. He was born in New Zealand but moved to the UK when he was a boy. We met at Eton. He was briefly married to Amber. I was best man at his wedding. I hope one day they will re-unite." He paused. "Is that enough to convince you I speak the truth?"

"That's more information than *I* know about him. I only joined the boat a few weeks ago."

"He'll vouch for my respectability." He pulled out his cell phone. "Do you wish to phone him?"

She certainly didn't. There would be hell to pay from the control freak of a captain who insisted on everybody doing as he said 24/7. Illicit midnight swims were definitely not on the roster.

"Okay. I buy it."

"Good. My name is Razeen." He stepped forward and she could see him more clearly.

"Razeen?" She frowned. "I've heard that name before. Is it a common one?"

"In Sitra it is."

"But you went to university in England; you sound English."

"I was educated in England from a young age but I am also a proud Sitran."

"I'm not surprised. It's a beautiful country."

"Have you seen much of it so far?"

"No, it's not exactly geared to tourists. But Alex has set something up for me in the capital so I hope to see more of it then."

He paused briefly. "Good."

"My name is Lucy. Lucy Gee."

She stepped forward and extended

her hand. His hand slid along her palm and curled around hers, warm and strong, gripping it with a sensuality that sent waves of heat through her body. His touch held a power she couldn't resist. She swayed imperceptibly closer to him, her fingers curling around his in response. Their hands were like two lit matches, melding together, unable to part. They just fitted together. She wondered if he felt the same as he continued to hold her hand for seconds longer than he should. Then he withdrew his hand, stepped away and looked across the bay. Perhaps she'd been wrong.

"So, would you like to see the bay's secret?"

She shuffled her feet. "I probably should be getting back."

"Of course, the decision is yours entirely. I, also, should be returning."

He waited for her response. She should leave but she didn't want to. It wasn't only that there was something compelling about this man that made her want to stay, it was more that she felt at some instinctive level, she could trust him. She'd been traveling non-stop for eight years and had often found herself in situations where she'd had to make instant decisions. Her instincts hadn't failed her during that time. Besides, she *wanted* to trust them now. She drew in a deep breath.

"Okay. Would you show me?"

Again the grin. "This way, Miss Gee." There was something about his formality, about the way the warm breeze tousled his hair and his shirt flapped lightly, which stimulated her more effectively than any overt flirtation. She shivered as a slick wave of attraction filtered through her body before settling in her gut. His grin disappeared into a frown. "You're cold?"

"No, I'm fine."

"Then come, I'll show you the hidden treasure of the bay."

As they walked, side by side along the water's edge, with the sea easing up and falling away from them with a sigh, and the palm trees softly clattering in the gentle wind, Lucy tried desperately to think of something to say. She drew a breath and turned to him, but the words evaporated when faced with his broad shoulders and dark gaze. She stared straight ahead again, toward the promontory.

"Aren't you curious about where we're going?"

'Curious' didn't begin to describe how she felt. She focused on calming her quickened heart. "Of course. Somewhere in front of us, I guess."

"You guess right." He pointed ahead of them. "You see where the promontory ends in a pile of rocks? Amongst them is a small sandy cove— it's in there."

"*What's* in there?"

She caught his gaze and his smile radiated a heat that wrapped around her whole body. "You mustn't be impatient. All will be revealed shortly. But there are clues already—you're walking on one."

"Umm, a mystery. Well, the sand's definitely warmer here. So…"

"You'll see."

He stopped suddenly and Lucy scanned the cliff face that from a distance appeared solid. It was only when she stood immediately before it, she could see that sharply overhanging rocks protruded over a recessed area. As they approached this recess, a twist in the rocks revealed a darkness unlit by the stars or the moon. She glanced at Razeen, suddenly uncertain.

He stopped at the entrance as if sensing her disquiet. "It's most beautiful at night but you're welcome to return by day if you prefer."

A brief argument raged in Lucy's head. She knew she shouldn't enter the caves at night with a stranger, of course she shouldn't. But when had she ever done anything correctly? She could look after herself. "Now is good. I want to see it at its best."

"Then take my hand and I'll lead you."

She peered ahead. "It's pitch black in there."

"I've been coming here since I was a boy. I know it inside out. Trust me."

"I guess there's a first time for everything." *Including trusting someone.*

She offered her hand and he clasped it and drew her after him, inside the narrow passage. They walked along a passage that twisted and turned as it penetrated deeper into the rocks. The heat increased, as did a smell that reminded Lucy of her childhood home in New Zealand—sulphur. There was a sharp twist in the path and the space suddenly opened out. They'd arrived.

"Wow…" Lucy exhaled in wonder as she shuffled round in a complete circle, her head lifted to absorb the pulsing light of thousands of glow-worms that clung to the rocks above the large, natural pool. "It's beautiful." She went to take a step forward.

"Careful," he grabbed her arm just as her foot slipped on the flat rocks that surrounded the pool. "It's deep."

The slight movement of his fingers on her arm as they lightly caressed her before he drew his hand away, raised the heat like no thermal spring could.

"But I have my bikini on."

He glanced at her breasts before meeting her gaze once more. "You want to go in?"

"If *you* do."

"I would have to go in without any clothes and I'm not sure you'd be comfortable with that." He smiled. "Am I right?"

Comfortable wasn't the word that immediately sprang to Lucy's mind. Interested was, intrigued, compelled. She'd never seen eyes like his. They were dark, melting and warm under the blue light of the cave—like chocolate, she thought. She licked her lips, almost feeling the effect of him on her tongue. She should walk out now. She should leave, swim back to the boat. But her body made no movement and the thoughts drifted away under the compulsion of his gaze. She sucked in a deep, steadying breath.

"Yeah. You *are* right. Let's just sit for a while. I'll need to return to the boat soon." She sat on the stone and sunk her feet into the warm water. "The glow-worms' lights are fading."

He sat beside her and put his legs into the water, ignoring the fact his trousers were getting wet. "Because we're disturbing them. We must speak quietly."

For a few moments they both looked around, watching as the blue-green lights sparked back into life again. It was a magical place. Steam escaped in tendrils through the cooler air, up above and out of the cave and into the moonlit sky high above them. She moved her feet through the water, watching the phosphorescence shimmer with each movement.

"Local legend has it that a sea monster lives here." His voice was a low whisper.

"I'm used to sea monsters," she whispered back. "We have them back home in New Zealand. The Maori call them *taniwha*. Seems every culture has some figment of their imagination to scare the heck out of them."

"Not of the imagination here. They are real enough to the people of my country."

"Yeah, right."

"Truly. Legend says that whoever

sees the *djullinar* will be forced to confront that which he, or she, most dreads."

A shiver ran down her spine. She didn't know if it was a result of his words or his warm breath against her cheek. "What happens if there's nothing you dread?"

"No one is totally unafraid."

"I am. Nothing can hurt me."

"That sounds like you've been hurt too much already."

The silence continued for too long but Lucy didn't know how to break it. No one had said anything like that to her for a long time. She went out of her way to appear invulnerable and most of the time succeeded. But, for some reason, this man saw through the resilient façade she'd created. She swallowed hard, trying to rid herself of the tension that had sprung to her temples. She forced herself to open her lips to speak but her throat was dry and she dared not trust her voice.

"I'm sorry, Lucy, I've no wish to pry. It was just an observation, no doubt an inaccurate one. Why don't you try out the water? You're shivering and the water will warm you."

Despite the warm air, she did suddenly feel cold and, glad of the diversion he'd given her, she slipped into the pool. Easing her legs into the hot water, she leaned back against the black rocks until her feet found a ledge. Then she sat on the submerged rock and relaxed as the warm water lapped around her shoulders.

"Oh my," she sighed. "This is worth the risk of a *taniwha*."

"Perhaps it's a trick of the *taniwha* to lure you closer to him. Lull you into a false sense of security before striking."

Despite the heat she shivered again. "I don't believe in monsters. Your monster is just something the owner invented to keep people out."

"So cynical. And so brave. What would warn you off, I wonder?"

"I guess everyone has their own *taniwha*. Something that makes them run. And mine is not a many-legged monster."

"No, I should imagine not. A young woman who would dive into a strange sea in the middle of the night and swim to a strange country, would not be frightened of such monsters. We do have sharks here, you know."

"Small ones. But not inside the reef— Alex told me. I'm not frightened of them anyway. When I was young, before my mother died, I used to go diving. I came across a small shark once, it came too close so I hit it on the nose and it went away."

He laughed and the sound swam into her body, warming and teasing her at the same time.

"You're a fearsome woman, Lucy. I hope you don't decide I'm your enemy and hit me on the nose."

Without thinking she turned in the water and reached up and touched his nose. His breath stilled at her touch and she didn't move.

She shook her head. "No, it's too nice a nose."

His hand caught hers and brought it to his lips. Then he kissed the palm of her hand and her breath caught in her throat.

"That's good to hear. I'm very fond of my nose."

She glanced at his nose and then back to his eyes. Somehow she'd moved closer to him until her body pressed lightly against his legs. It seemed entirely natural when his other hand curled around her cheek.

"Where on earth did you come from, Miss Gee?" His breath was warm on her face, heating her skin and seeping down inside her body.

"From the sea, like your own

taniwha."

"But one should run from one's monsters, not embrace them."

"One doesn't always do what one should."

"Indeed." He held her hand tight against his chest and she could feel his heart beat as rapidly as hers. Then his hand slid through her wet hair and brought her face to his. She closed her eyes as her body relaxed against his. When his lips touched hers it came as no surprise, no shock, simply a spreading warmth of familiarity. It was as if her body had been needing, searching for, this man's touch her whole life.

His lips were more powerful, more possessive upon hers, than she'd imagined. He was so proper and courteous, despite the sensuality she sensed in him, that she hadn't imagined that he'd so expertly capture her mouth. But he did. His lips held hers, moving against and opening hers until the slow burn low in her body caught and ignited. She gasped against his mouth and felt his breathing quicken.

Slowly he slid into the water and pulled her tight against him, drawing her close until their bodies were molded one against the other. The buttons on his shirt dug into her breasts and stomach, the silky material slid against her bare skin. The heat of his body against hers was hotter than the thermal waters. He was like fire—fire playing with fire.

She put her arms around him, exploring his muscles through his wet shirt, before pushing the material out of the way, so she could feel the texture and heat of his skin directly against her own skin. Her mind drifted into a sensory heaven. There was no longer any thought of who they were, of what they were doing there—there was only feeling. And it was a feeling she wanted to intensify. He groaned and for one instant she pressed her hips close to his and felt his hardness, before he pulled away.

"Lucy." His voice was husky with desire.

"Umm…" She sought his lips again, not wanting to surrender that sense of completeness. His hands felt like bliss against her starved skin. She held her face close to his, her lips a kiss away from his own, inviting him, enticing him.

"Lucy." Her name sounded like a caress against her mouth. But slowly, he let his hands fall from her back until they rested loosely around her waist. He shook his head and moved away until he was no longer touching her.

She gazed into his dark eyes, eyes that reflected the myriad lights from around the cave. "What is it?" She hardly recognized the low, husky voice as her own.

"This isn't right." He shook his head. "Look at you. I would be taking complete advantage of you here, alone, wearing so little."

"But—"

His finger touched her lips briefly. "No. It's not right."

Slowly the beat of her heart settled and the truth of his words sunk in. She closed her eyes tight at the thought of how the kiss might have progressed.

She shook her head. "I'm sorry, I don't know what I was thinking." She hadn't behaved so rashly since she was a teenager when she'd been full of rage and desperate for affection. Nothing good could come from it. She knew that for a fact.

"Neither of us was thinking straight. I'm a stranger to you now, but I don't intend to be one. I'll see you again."

"You sound so sure."

"I am. I *will* see you again and we will take up where we left off tonight. But here, now, we must leave it."

Razeen was like no man she'd ever met before—so caring, so intent on doing the right thing. Lucy frowned and turned away uncertainly.

"Are you sure you like me?"

That laugh again. "Quite sure. But now isn't the right time."

She smiled and her fingers found their way to his chest. "You're right. Thank you."

"I don't want you to have any doubts; I don't want you to regret this." Her smile faded. She knew she wouldn't regret it but she also knew that she wouldn't be seeing him again. She'd be gone from the bay in the morning. "Come, it'll soon be dawn." He lifted her onto the ledge of the pool and pushed himself back out after her. He took her hands and rose, lifting her to her feet at the same time. "You should be getting back to the boat."

She looked around, forcing herself

to re-focus, to pull away from the intensity she'd experienced with this stranger. "Yes, of course." She glanced down at her bikini-clad body and then back at him. "I'm sorry, I don't usually do this sort of thing." She gave an embarrassed laugh. "There must be something in the air here in Sitra."

"Maybe, or perhaps it's us. I'll see you again, Lucy, and then we'll find out whether it's the night air, or us."

She shook her head slightly, so slightly that he wouldn't know she was declining. It had to have been here and now, or nothing. Lucy Gee didn't do relationships. She wouldn't be seeing him again. Once she reached the city of Sitra she'd be leaving the team. She had a mission of her own to accomplish in that city.

He took her hand and they made their way through the dark tunnel, back to the beach once more. The soft, filmy light of dawn filled the sky. She scanned the beach and could now see what she'd failed to see in the darkness of the night—a lone vehicle parked beyond the trees that fringed the beach.

"Your car."

"Yes." In the pale peachy light he seemed less real to her than he had in the dark, when sight was the least of the senses that had drawn her to him. He was a stranger now. She let her hand slip from his. He must have felt some of what passed through her because the expression in his eyes appeared to harden a little as he stepped away from her.

"Your boat," he glanced toward the Explorer, now also clearly visible.

She nodded. "They'll be waking soon and will want their breakfast." She couldn't drag her eyes away from him, his damp clothes clinging to every contour of his muscled body. She could see he was still thinking of her, that his body still wanted her. "Thank you for tonight. It was beautiful."

"Your hair is curling now it's beginning to dry."

"It has a mind of its own."

"Like you."

"Like me." She stepped away, backwards at first before turning and running into the sea.

He watched as she ran, the flimsy purple bikini that he'd spent so much time contemplating, barely covering her slim hips and full breasts. Then she turned and waved as the swell of a wave surged around her, covering her body and shoulders with water, before she turned back and dived into the water and was gone: arms swiftly taking her back to the boat.

He'd said he'd see her again. And he would. She didn't know it, but they already had an appointment.

CHAPTER TWO

Lucy traced the line of her sister's face on the iPad. There was nothing unusual about the slightly out-of-focus photograph—beautiful designer clothes, expensive smile, on the arm of a handsome man—only the best for Maia. No, the unusual thing was that it was the last photo she'd seen of her in four months, the last photo her sister had posted on Facebook.

Where are you, Maia?

Lucy scrolled up the page, skimming over the more recent messages Maia had supposedly posted, and frowned. The messages had definitely been written by Maia—no one else could have known the details she posted—but they weren't current. Maia hadn't been where she said she'd been. Lucy knew because she'd checked. She'd been to the places where Maia was supposed to have been and no one had seen her. Also, Maia wasn't replying to any messages or comments, which wasn't like her.

They'd made two pacts with each other as teenagers: one, to live life to the full and the other, to stay in contact. They were, after all, the only family each other had. Hence Facebook, hence Twitter. But for some reason Maia had stopped keeping in touch. Lucy wasn't fooled by the recent updates. Something had happened to Maia and her only clue was this last photo: of Maia with the King of Sitra.

Lucy carefully tucked away the iPad into her rucksack and wished she could put away her concern as easily. Her fears for Maia were always with her, like a sharp tension running through her body. She swung the bag on her back and stepped out onto the deck.

They were sailing around the outer point of Sitra harbor. As they inched around the lighthouse that clung to the rocks, the pristine coastline gave way to the rambling terra cotta and sand-colored buildings of the medieval city of Sitra. The soft earth tones of the city's buildings were interspersed with the grey-greens of date palms, pomegranate and fig trees, revealing the city's oasis origins. The fresh water and strategic coastal position had made it a key port in the export of incense to the Mediterranean and India. Now, it was a backwater of outdated systems—a country rife with intrigue. And somewhere amidst the maze of winding streets, of ancient buildings and robe-swathed people, was her sister.

Where was she? Who was she with?

Was she being held against her will? Either Maia was holding back the truth or someone was preventing her from communicating with Lucy. The thought made her sick to her stomach. She had to find her. Lucy's mind drifted back to the photo of Maia and the King. It was all she had to go on.

A low wolf whistle drew her attention to Alex, the captain. She grinned and did a twirl, allowing the soft folds of one of her few dresses to swing around her legs. She knew the white of the dress contrasted well with her deep tan. Then she let her sunglasses tip down her nose and peered over them in a come-hither look she'd seen her sister practice many times.

"Well, don't you scrub up well? Still wearing your old compass though. Never know when you'll need it, eh?"

Lucy fingered the antique compass that she always wore on a chain around her neck, one of the few reminders of her mother, and turned to Alex with a smile. He was leaning against the railings of the boat watching the city slowly draw near. She wandered over to him and leaned back against the railings. He ruffled her hair out of her carefully prepared French twist and she grinned. He might be a control freak with the rest of the crew but outside work hours he treated her like a kid sister and he felt like the brother she'd never had.

"Don't want to get lost out there."

"I don't think you're someone who gets lost easily. Anyhow, you look lovely."

"Why, thank you. Thought I'd better look my best for the King."

"Good idea, but you're wearing the wrong clothes. If you want to stay here a while, you need to get on the right side of the King and his people. What you need to do is wear this." He passed her the robe that he'd slung over one shoulder. "I thought you wouldn't be prepared."

"A burqa?"

"No, the black coat is called an abaya and you wear this scarf—it's called a hijab—over your hair. As a non-Muslim you don't need to cover up with a burqa."

"But—" spluttered Lucy.

"When in Rome, Luce."

"But I'm not in Rome, I'm here—"

"In a Muslim country. Exactly. If you want to get a stamp on your passport you'll need the King's support. Nothing goes on around here without his knowledge, or approval. If you want the King's support, wear this."

She sighed and took the robe. "I just thought with the King's reputation that I'd be able to wear what I liked."

Alex laughed. "Inside the palace, yes. But outside? No." He squinted at the horizon. "See over there, on top of the ridge, that long white building? That's the palace."

Lucy narrowed her eyes, intent on focusing on the building, until her eyes watered with the effort. Had her sister stayed there? Or had she somehow disappeared into the sprawling city. There were many questions but she knew only one fact. Alex's words echoed in her mind.

Nothing went on without the King's knowledge. Nothing.

The small car wove its way carefully through the narrow streets of the old city. The stone walls of the merchant houses, painted soft shades of ochre, terra cotta and lime white, were peeling in places. Small shops opened out onto the street displaying the kinds of goods that had been traded for millennia: incense such as frankincense and myrrh from Sitra itself, spices from India and silks from China. The smell of freshly baked bread drifted into the car from the many street stalls, making Lucy's mouth water. It was a long time since breakfast and she'd been up most of the night.

Despite trying to focus on what was before her, her mind lingered on the man she'd met on the beach. Just the thought of him sent flutters into her stomach. He'd said they'd meet again but she couldn't see how they would. He knew the name of her boat, knew her captain, but that was all. No one knew her real purpose in coming to Sitra. And that's the way it had to be.

It was curiosity only that had made her try to elicit information from Alex earlier that morning. But it hadn't been forthcoming and she hadn't dared to press it. For all his kindness to her, he was a stickler for rules and his "no swimming at night" rule was non negotiable. Her reveries were suddenly interrupted by a sharp shove in her ribs.

"As much as I hate to stop the day dreams that seem to having such a pleasurable effect on you, we're here."

Lucy followed Alex and the others out of the car and into a large, formal courtyard. Here, the heat of the morning sun was filtered through a tracery of branches interwoven to form an overhead canopy to protect visitors. A phalanx of white-gowned men awaited them. All tall, armed and wearing stony expressions, they were obviously designed to impress and intimidate—and they did. Lucy was glad she was wearing the abaya now. It gave her a feeling of protection, something she could hide behind.

Their small group was ushered through the massive, solid double doors and into an empty hall, where the slap of their sandals and shoes echoed too loudly. Lucy's heart thumped heavily in her chest and sweat trickled down her back. It was far more formal, far more awe-inspiring than she'd imagined. They waited for several minutes in the hall until they received a signal from a guard who opened an adjoining door. They entered the vast reception room and were ushered over to a group of rococo gilt-edged chairs ranged at one end. The room was filled with ornate furniture, and magnificent paintings and priceless rugs covered the marble floor.

"You may wait here."

They sat on the chairs that were grouped around a low table, opposite one empty chair, and looked around.

Lucy's heart thumped in her chest. Four months of planning, sixteen weeks of worry, one hundred and twelve days of waiting, to meet the only known lead she had to her sister's whereabouts, were finally over. The heavy tick of an over-sized clock marked the passage of long minutes as the others, who also appeared tense, fidgeted.

"Do you think he'll give us permission to continue the research?" whispered the lead scientist.

Alex shrugged as he glanced around at the paintings. "Maybe. Although the Sheikh's got enough on his plate here—"

"Sheikh? I thought he was a King?"

Alex grinned at Lucy. "He is King. We used to call him 'the sheikh' at school—it used to really piss him off."

Lucy frowned. "At school? How many people do you know in Sitra?"

It was Alex's turn to frown but anything he was about to say was interrupted by one of his team.

"So what do you reckon the chances are we'll receive permission?"

"As I was saying, although he's busy sorting out the country he's inherited—he's still committed to preserving the environment, and the reef in particular. It could be a big tourism earner for the country eventually."

"Money!" Lucy scoffed. "It always comes down to money—so mercenary."

A deeper hush descended on them and Lucy felt a prickle up her spine and a light sheen of sweat bloom over her body. The expression on the lead scientist's face was one of sheer panic. Alex's deep frown lightened immediately and turned into a wide grin. The faint rustle of robes turned into the whisper of soft shoes against marble as footsteps moved behind her and up to the chair on the other side of the low table.

Lucy closed her eyes with embarrassment and regret. She hadn't heard the silent advance of the King and his party. What a way to start. What a way to repay Alex for all his kindness to her. When she opened her eyes she found two bodyguards, standing either side of the empty chair, staring at her disapprovingly. She swung round to see Alex and a robed figure hugging each other, clapping each other on the back. The sun caught the white silk folds of the man's robes that fell in undulating ripples from broad shoulders. Then he turned and eyes as dark as chocolate held hers with an intensity and curiosity that took her breath away.

She gasped and studied the floor in panic, as memories of the man she'd met in the night merged with the man who now moved slowly toward her as Alex introduced him to the team, one by one.

He'd known. All along, he'd known that they'd meet again. She'd told him they were meeting the King the next day. So he'd known, but hadn't said anything. She recalled the night's events slowly, as if flicking through photographs, as she tried to remember what had been said, what had been done. But her mind didn't move beyond the kiss as her body responded just as it had in the night.

She kept her eyes lowered and bowed, just as she'd been told to do. But she couldn't stop her nostrils flaring to catch the deep leathery tones of his aftershave, so masculine, so reminiscent of the stranger she'd met on the beach. She could feel the King's eyes upon her, their force keeping her head bowed.

"And this is Lucy Gee, a fellow New Zealander," Alex said. She looked up to find the King standing before her, an amused expression on his face. "It's Lucy's culinary expertise that's kept us going. She's a nutrition nut and had us eating all the healthy stuff.' Alex grinned at Lucy and glanced at the King expectantly. But there were no words of welcome as he'd uttered to the others. Instead there was a long pause during which Alex's puzzled expression moved first from one amused face to the other, blushing face. It was the amused face that spoke first.

"Welcome to our country, Lucy." His voice was the same as Lucy remembered and had the same effect, like notes playing softly upon her skin, the vibrations continuing into her body.

"You two haven't met before, have you?"

"And how could we have done that, Alex?" The King's lips quirked into a smile and he dipped his head to Lucy before turning away. "Knowing how tight a ship you run, I'm sure Lucy hasn't had the time or opportunity to leave the boat."

The King turned away and walked over to the vacant chair, either side of which a bodyguard stood. Now he'd drawn away from her he was entirely the King. She could hardly reconcile the man before her with the man from last night. His power and status were palpable. Besides the guards, there were attendants at all the doors, a secretary hovering near and domestic staff placing refreshments before them.

He waved his hand. "Please, be seated."

They sat in the ornate chairs and Lucy willed herself to relax. She inhaled deeply but the dry air caught in her throat, making her cough. She glanced up at him, only to discover he was staring directly at her. His dark eyes appeared cold under the harsh light of the reception room, his brow was lowered and the sharp planes of his cheeks fell in shadows to a mouth that seemed more thoughtful than passionate. She immediately lowered her eyes and thanked God for the custom of women keeping their eyes lowered. Normally she would have balked at the restriction, but now? She was intensely grateful for it, as she studied the ancient patterns within the marble floor. She needed time to think and only half-listened to the polite conversation the King conducted with the crew, and the more playful banter he exchanged with Alex.

Could this be the man who was somehow implicated in Maia's disappearance? This man, whom she'd nearly made love to last night but who'd carefully extricated himself with cool control, despite what his body had so obviously wanted? This was the monster she'd come to investigate? She sipped the mint tea she'd been given as she tried to comprehend the impossible. Had Maia been seduced as easily as she'd nearly been?

"Lucy! Answer the King."

Lucy looked up, bewildered. "I'm sorry…"

The King leaned forward toward her, his arms on his knees. The increased proximity was all it took to bring the flood of color to her cheeks once more. "I understand from Alex that you wish is to stay here for a short holiday rather than proceed with the expedition."

She nodded, not knowing if her voice would be steady.

"I was asking, Miss Gee, if you would care to stay here at the palace, as my guest."

Lucy swallowed. It was more than she could have hoped for. It was being handed to her on a plate. Except for one thing. She hadn't anticipated, in her wildest dreams, that she would *want* the man on whom all her suspicions were focused. Not just want, but physically ache for him.

"That," she cleared her throat of the huskiness that was threatening to creep into it, "would be very, er, agreeable." She glanced quickly at Alex who sat back in his chair, one hand tapping his lips, amusement brimming in his eyes as he glanced between Lucy and the King. "Thank you. If that's okay with you Alex?"

"Certainly." He smiled slyly at the

King. "We'll miss Lucy but I can recruit a replacement here—with your help. I know Lucy will be in good hands, so to speak."

The King's expression didn't change, his eyes remained on Lucy, either oblivious to, or determined to ignore, the innuendo in Alex's words. "Then, Lucy, you are most welcome."

The low tone of his voice filtered through her body like a vibration: from the bones in her feet, sweeping up through the heat at her centre and out to her fingertips. Suddenly panic gripped her. She was totally susceptible to him. What the hell did she think she was doing? Was she mad? Did she really believe she could find Maia in this world—closed for so long to outsiders—or would she more likely end up the same way as her sister? Disappear in this hot southern land without trace?

"Are you sure it's not an imposition?"

He gestured around him. "The palace is vast. It's no imposition."

"But…"

"But, what? You think perhaps I require payment for my hospitality? Such an attitude would be called 'mercenary', do you not think, Miss Gee?"

So he had heard.

"I…I'm sorry. I didn't mean to—"

He waved his hand as if to brush away her apology. "You were correct in one regard. I do want something from you."

The continual thrumming sensation inspired by his proximity suddenly turned to fear. She bit her lip to try to stem the trembling as she met his thoughtful gaze. "And what's that?" Her voice sounded falsely loud to her over-sensitive ears.

"My country has no tourism industry. I wish to develop one—carefully and on a small scale—and Alex tells me you have a background in the hospitality industry. I'd be interested in your opinion on how to develop the tourism projects we have planned."

She exhaled a tense breath and suddenly felt calmer. She was on surer, more familiar ground now. "I'm no expert but I've traveled widely. I'd be happy to give you informal advice."

"Perfect. You may stay here at the palace as long as you wish and I will arrange a guide to show you around. I have someone in mind." The heat of his brown eyes bridged the space between them and she flicked her tongue around suddenly needy lips. His gaze dipped to her mouth and stayed there, for one long moment, before returning to her eyes, the chocolate brown of his eyes now darker than before, as if burned by the heat. He recovered swiftly and the heat was replaced by a flicker of humor, reinforced by a slight crinkling of the fine lines at the outer corners of his eyes. She felt the visceral stab of lust, low in her body. It ground in deep and refused to leave.

"Thank you." She hesitated as she racked her brain for something normal to say, something that wouldn't reveal her body's response to him. "Your country appears very beautiful. I'm interested in seeing as much as possible." He frowned. She could have kicked herself. She was so busy trying to cover her reaction to this powerful man that she'd made him suspicious.

"Any particular reason?"

"I write the occasional travel piece. The magazine editor's keen for one on a country few know anything about."

"My father's decision to isolate our country from the West was no doubt the best one at the time. But times have changed. I think your reports could be very helpful to us. Is there anything in particular you wish to know?"

What the hell's happened to my

sister? Lucy sucked in a raw breath—the dry air-conditioned air ripping through her lungs. "Sitra's heritage, its culture, of course, and also the kind of things that could attract a twenty-first-century tourist. Someone like me." *Someone like Maia.*

"I will show you around personally, and my staff will make sure you have everything you require."

"Thank you. That's very kind."

"Kind?" The repeated word was softly spoken, barely breathed, but it sent shivers of anticipation skittering up and down her spine as she contemplated what it was the King would gain from this personal attention. "I'm sure I will enjoy it. Alex, perhaps you'd send Miss Gee's things to the palace."

Alex was sitting back in his chair, arms crossed, unable to stop a grin from spreading across his face. "Sure."

The King's eyes never left hers and Lucy's heart raced; heat shimmered through her body, despite the air conditioning, and it felt as if they were the only two people in the room. And then he smiled: his lips quirking briefly at the corners, as if in both acknowledgement of their unspoken exchange, and of dismissal. He shifted in his seat and turned to Alex, talking amiably as if nothing had happened.

It was as if the sun had dipped below the horizon, leaving her alone in darkness. She turned around to see if anyone had noticed her sudden vulnerability—she was never vulnerable, she was always the strong one—but everyone else was focused on the conversation between Alex and the King. They were all too caught up with the opportunity to continue their work, researching the reef and marine life off the coast of Sitra. None of the others had noticed the intensity of their exchange. For a brief moment she wondered if it had been all in her imagination. But no, a quick, curious glance from the King and she saw she hadn't imagined any of it.

She focused on her hands that were tightly clasped in her lap and let the conversation flow over her as she tried to contain the deep-seated guilt that stirred in the pit of her stomach. She was lusting after someone who was implicated in the disappearance of her sister. She'd thought she'd anticipated every eventuality but this had never occurred to her. Her mind was set— she had to find out what happened to Maia. But her body swayed, drawn by this stranger's scent, mesmerized by his eyes, melting under his touch. She wrung her hands together more tightly, desperate for control. The last image her sister had posted on Facebook floated into her mind—a beaming smile for the paparazzi as she leaned into the embrace of a tall, dark man—the King of Sitra.

Suddenly she realized the talk had come to an end. She looked up to see people were standing as the King made arrangements to see Alex in a few weeks' time. The crew came to say their farewells to Lucy and she embraced Alex, reluctantly drawing away but still holding onto his hands, unwilling to let go, suddenly scared. Alex frowned and drew her to one side.

"You okay, Luce?"

She drew in a deep breath and nodded too vigorously. "Sure."

"Come back with us if you want," he whispered. "But, you know, the King's a good man. You'll be safe in his hands. I've known him since we were seven years old. Your choice."

She was filled with gratitude for the kindness of this man whom she'd only known a few weeks. "I'll be fine. Just feeling a bit hot under these robes." She grinned. "Thanks, Alex, for everything. I'll be okay. It's what I want."

He grinned. "You'll be fine. You have my phone number if you need me." He squeezed her hands in his and walked over to his team who were talking with the King. When they'd finished, the King stepped back to where his bodyguards stood. It was a signal the audience was at an end. He swept out of the room without a second glance at Lucy. People disappeared from the many doors that lined the reception room and after a few hugs and farewells, Lucy watched her friends disappear to attend the meetings the King had arranged with his own team of scientists.

As her colleagues left the room, part of her wanted to run after them and cling to them and beg them to take her back with them. But that part was the coward who'd let Maia step in front of her and defend her against school bullies. The same scared part that would watch as Maia lied to authorities about who looked after them. Maia had had no qualms about such things; she'd believed she was quite capable of looking after her little sister—Maia had been sixteen after all.

But that was then and this was now.

Maia had brought her up and brought her up strong. And she had to be strong now, for her. She turned around to see a woman waiting discreetly behind her. The woman bowed, waiting for Lucy to come with her. She had no choice; she had to find Maia. She smiled uncertainly and went over to the waiting woman.

Alex and the research team may have got what they needed from the King but, for her, the quest was only just beginning.

CHAPTER THREE

Razeen tried to focus on his advisor's report on the economic reforms he'd implemented, but his mind was full of the woman in the black abaya, whose eyes held a challenge and attraction like none he could remember.

"Your Majesty, everything is on track, but—"

His advisor's hesitation brought Razeen's mind back to his current problems. "None of it's working, is it?"

His advisor examined the papers in his hands. "No, Your Majesty, it's not. Everything is in place; on paper the systems and procedures are workable but, the people... the people are not yet behind it."

Razeen sighed. "And until they are, we don't stand a chance of implementing these reforms, do we?"

The advisor shook his head in silent agreement.

"What is it they want?"

The advisor coughed. "Your Majesty…"

Razeen winced at the title. His attempts at informality within the palace had been met with stony resistance and he'd soon returned to the formality of his father's reign.

"Najib, just tell me what you think will work, tell me how you believe we can move on from here. You knew my father, you knew my brother, what would they have done?"

The older man, his weathered face settled in deep vertical lines, pushed up his spectacles and peered at Razeen, blinking. His intelligent, astute eyes were full of doubt. Razeen understood the doubt. Both his father and brother had been raised to take on the traditional role of King of their country. Razeen hadn't.

"The people want a King who is a true leader—a sheikh. The people need reform—*that* you have given them—but they want a traditional sheikh, with a traditional family. *Then*, I believe they will accept the reforms."

"A traditional family," Razeen scoffed. "A traditional wife you mean. I've been seen in every tabloid newspaper, in every country, with every new model on my arm. I'm not exactly known for tradition."

"I do not believe the people will care. In fact, someone who turns their back on the West in favor of traditional values will be seen to validate their way of life. Give them yourself, reformed, and you can bring the country into the twenty-first century, you can bring prosperity to the people once more."

"Myself, reformed."

He closed his eyes and tried to rid himself of the image of green eyes, a heart-shaped face and wayward strands of sun-streaked honey-brown hair that had escaped the hijab; he tried to eradicate the memory of her lips upon his, but it didn't work. He opened his eyes, feeling anger and frustration in every cell of his body at what might have been. But "what might have been"—his ability to choose what he wanted from life—had died along with his brother.

"Myself, married." Of all the things he'd anticipated in the first twenty-eight years of his life, an arranged marriage was not one of them. "I suppose I'm unable to choose."

"Of course you may choose. We have already compiled a selection for you to choose from." The old man's eyes lit up with excitement. "It is the best decision, Your Majesty. There are a number of young women from the most distinguished Sitran families who would be suitable. Their alliance would guarantee you support from key tribes. It will be the most effective strategy you can adopt to secure your country's future."

Razeen rose and walked over to the window overlooking the city. It lay, spread before him, its subtle tones of sand and terra cotta sharply juxtaposed against the stunning brilliance of the aqua sea. But the beauty was a mask to the corruption and disorganization that was crippling his country's wealth. The only way forward was to gain the support of the people with the power—the country's old elite—and the affection of a people whose life was centered on tradition. The only way.

"Make the arrangements." His mind flicked back to Lucy once more. She was here now. She'd be gone within weeks and he'd be left with years of duty and responsibility. "But I want my diary cleared of all but the most urgent meetings for two weeks." He sighed deeply, feeling the burden of his duty more oppressively than he'd ever done before. "No functions, no introductions, no meetings other than essential ones, for two weeks." His advisor bowed his head in acceptance. And Razeen closed his eyes in regret.

Lucy was filled by a sense of both beauty and isolation as the servant led the way to her room. It was a world within a world. From the symmetry and control of the formal wing of the palace—with its over-sized marble fountains and clipped trees—to the older, more rambling parts of the palace, there was a quietness, a remoteness, which made Lucy uneasy.

She had the weird feeling that she might just disappear amongst the maze of colonnaded walkways, perfumed gardens and darkened doorways and never reappear. She shivered. Had Maia been here? Had she felt the same? Had she smelt these same fragrances? Had she also tasted the lips of the sheikh?

Lucy felt the chill ache of poisonous self-recriminations in every fiber of her body. True, she hadn't known his identity, but equally true she'd been a fool: too confident in her own ability to survive and too impetuous as usual. And she'd berated her sister for her impulsive ways. Lucy was as bad.

The servant stopped suddenly beside a large wooden door. "Here, madam. Here is your room."

"Thank you."

"If you need anything, please use the telephone. Please call at any time."

"Any internet access?"

"No, madam. Only the office and the King have access to the internet."

"Really?" Lucy couldn't prevent incredulity from creeping into her voice.

"It was not something we had in this country until the new King took the throne."

Lucy thought the woman's tone sounded faintly disapproving. "You don't know what you've been missing."

The woman, for all her supposed lowly status, gazed pityingly at Lucy. "We managed well without it." She paused briefly to collect herself. "If you wish to go anywhere, please use the telephone. Someone will come for you."

"Thanks but I'm sure I won't be needing you. I'll find my own way about."

"No, you must not do that. You could lose yourself."

Or go where I'm not wanted, thought Lucy.

"Please call and either myself," continued the maid, "or someone else will show you around, as you require. Until someone comes, you must wait."

"Thank you," Lucy replied ambiguously. She had no intention of calling anyone.

The woman retreated noiselessly on her soft sandals and Lucy entered the room, closing the door firmly behind her before leaning back on it and sighing with relief.

'Room' wasn't a word she'd have used to describe it. A small apartment was what she'd have called it. Being part of the older buildings the ceiling wasn't as lofty as in the newer wing of the palace, but the decor was fabulous. The floor was covered with ancient grey and white geometric tiles that continued up the first quarter of the wall. Above them the stone walls were creamy white. Simple white curtains and fabrics swathed the windows and four-poster bed. But it was the view that attracted Lucy's attention.

She walked across the room and opened the narrow French windows, revealing a small secluded garden onto which only her room led. On two sides, stone walls rose, covered in climbing plants, and on the fourth side a trellised wall backed onto what appeared to be an orchard. Within it was a small door. Here, the sounds of the palace and the city were muffled and distant, insignificant besides the soporific trickle of water that ran from a simple white marble spout before splitting into four rills of water that intersected the intricate tile pattern laid on the ground. Its geometric design was calming, as was the low, green light, from the sheltering canopy of interwoven trees above. It was simple, relaxing and magical.

She didn't want magical. She didn't want to be seduced either by a tall, dark, dangerous man, or by her surroundings. She wasn't used to luxury and she was scared of it: scared she'd be beguiled by it. She shook her head, as if to shed it of the lulling sound of the water, of the soft touch of the silk curtains beneath her fingers. She had to be strong—strong for Maia.

She skirted the seductive bed and sat on the upright chair in front of the small Louis XVI escritoire. She pulled the scarf from her head, pushed her fingers through her hair and held her head in her hands, as she tried to contain the conflicting feelings and thoughts that bombarded her. She *had* to focus.

She groaned. On one hand just the sight of this man whose lips she could still feel on her own, just the smell of his aftershave and his own masculine scent, just the feel of his presence had her body on fire for him. Yet on the other hand, this was the man who was her last clue to her sister's whereabouts. Quite possibly, he was dangerous. She couldn't let herself fall for him. And yet she couldn't avoid him. She needed him to trust her; she needed him to like her. Yet she knew she could be burned if she came too close. But she had no choice.

She jumped up and paced across the room. She had to get moving, *do* something. She couldn't just sit around and wait like some passive victim. She hadn't been able to access the internet for a few days and she was desperate to check to see if there were any more Facebook messages from Maia. Even if they had been designed to obscure where she was, at least they told her she was still alive. She needed to find an office.

She pulled the scarf back over her head, figuring it would at least give her a degree of anonymity, and stepped outside her suite of rooms. She cast quick glances around her, wondering which way to go. The gardens and covered walkways were empty and there was no sound to guide her. She didn't have a clue, but rather than return the way she'd come, she decided to explore deeper into the castle, taking the worn steps higher up the hill. Within moments she was lost and she realized why the maid had been so insistent upon her calling for someone. She'd imagined it was for control but she had to admit, as she came upon another set of doors that appeared identical to the last, she was hopelessly lost.

She retraced her steps until she reckoned she was close by her room. She pushed open a large door and found herself in an old, echoing hall that was sumptuously furnished. She listened for subdued voices, for any sign of life. But all was strangely quiet. Suddenly she felt nervous, as though she was intruding, and exited the rooms through open windows. Under the canopy of trees and tracery of greenery the mid-afternoon heat was tolerable. Here, the heavy scent of flowers was mediated by the salty tang of the sea, drifting to her on the soft breeze.

She paused for a moment, soaking up the atmosphere and then she saw a western newspaper left untidily on a cushioned seat designed for comfort rather than show. She looked closer and saw stereo speakers hidden in the trees. Her heart thumped heavily in her chest. She had to get out of here.

She turned abruptly, about to flee, but caught sight of someone alone, pacing the floor, hands thrust into his pockets, turning and then stopping before the open vista of the city below. It was Razeen; it was the King. Lucy froze. No wonder it was so quiet. This was obviously his private wing of the palace. She should move, she knew she had to leave, but there was something about him that compelled her to stay. This was not the man she'd seen earlier. There was a sense of despair, rather than of omnipotent power about him; a sense of sadness and loneliness, rather than confidence. The feelings she'd been so carefully trying to contain unraveled instantly. She only just managed to contain a gasp before turning away. But in her haste she caught her robes on a thorn of a bougainvillea and the sound of tearing cloth rent the air.

"Lucy!"

That voice! It sent ripples of longing through her. She drew in a deep breath, suddenly aware that the air had left her body. She turned to see him walking toward her with a haste prompted by either anger or the same need she felt. She didn't know which.

"Lucy, what are you doing here?" Within seconds he was beside her.

"Trying to walk around like a normal person swathed from head to foot in cloth that seems to catch everywhere."

He grinned. "Here, let me help you." He focused on untwisting the thorn from her robe. His large hands were gentle and he was so close that every one of her senses was aware of him: she was unable to take her eyes off the strong, downward sweep of his jawline. The brush of his fine robes against the back of her hand as his fingers twisted the cloth away from the grasping thorn sent shivers tracking through her body. The subtle smell of his aftershave, together with something indefinable, something purely him, fed her body with a stimulus she could do without.

"You knew," she whispered.

"I know many things—to what in particular are you referring?"

"That you'd be seeing me this morning."

"Of course. I would never have let you go otherwise."

A thrill ran through her body, despite everything she'd been trying to make herself think, make herself control. It all evaporated in his presence.

"You would have kept me with you by force?"

He frowned but his eyes glittered with amusement. "You think I am a savage from a savage country? Is that it Miss Gee?" He brought the tangled piece of cloth closer until it stroked her face.

"Not savage, just different. I don't know your ways."

"But you will. All I meant was, if I hadn't known I would see you again, I wouldn't have let you go without discovering how to contact you."

"Why? You can't be short of entertainment here. You're a King after all."

"Shall we say 'entertainment' alone can wear a little thin after a while? Besides you will prove useful to me. As I will to you, I hope."

She swallowed, trying to control the quickened thudding of her heart. His words were ambiguous, given what little she knew of Maia's last movements.

"What exactly is it you want from me?"

He shook his head, smiling and released her robes. "There, you are free from the thorn now." But he didn't step away. "And as to what I want from you?" He hesitated as he searched her face, as if looking for an answer to his own question. "*That* is an interesting question. And probably irrelevant."

It was her turn to show confusion. "I don't understand."

"My dear Lucy, what I want and what I allow myself are two different things. I am a ruler of a country; my life is not as simple as yours."

"Mine, simple?" she half-laughed. "Now I *know* you don't know me."

"No, of course. However, what I'd like from you is just as we'd discussed earlier. I need to bring my country into the twenty-first century and I need help to do it. Your knowledge of tourism, your magazine articles could prove invaluable."

"Surely you have experts who can help. I don't claim to be an authority."

"It's not only your experience. You are also the demographic we hope to entice here. It's one thing talking to an expert with theoretical knowledge, it's another talking to a young woman who's worked at the top dive spots in the world."

"Alex told you that?"

"Yes. Last night, before I met you, he told me about you, about your desire to stay for a few weeks to look around. So I was interested in you working for me." He paused. "But that was before I met you."

"And now?"

"After last night? I don't want you just for your expertise. I'd like to get to know you better. If that's also what you want?"

She wanted to scream two

contradictory answers. Instead she opened her mouth to speak but no words came. She simply nodded her agreement.

"Good. Now, perhaps I can offer you a cold drink and you can tell me more about yourself, about why you're here."

Again, all she could do was nod and follow him to the al fresco seating area where he poured her a glass of lemonade. "There's not much to tell, nothing interesting."

"Believe me, I'm interested. First, tell me, why did you come to Sitra?"

She was suddenly jolted back into reality. She could be honest and tell him straight answer, ask him outright if he knew were Maia was. But what if he was implicated and his answer was a blank "no"? She'd have lost her advantage. He'd throw her out of the country and she'd never be allowed back in. If he wasn't implicated and he was willing to help, he'd still be willing after she'd made some preliminary enquiries. She couldn't afford to lose her advantage. But she knew he wouldn't believe anything that had absolutely no foundation of truth.

"I've traveled a lot, catering on yachts, and love diving, especially in unspoiled places like here. When I saw the advert for working on Alex's expedition I was drawn to it. I knew entry into the country was impossible otherwise; I thought I might never get another chance."

"Hopefully you will. And others will too, if my plans work out."

"And what are your plans exactly?"

"Develop a few heavily protected diving resorts away from the capital city. The work Alex and his crew are doing will provide the ground work so we can both protect and promote the reefs."

"You've certainly got the beautiful beaches that will attract people. And the waters, they're so clear and warm. You'll have more problems keeping people away, I should think."

"Possibly. But Alex seems to think the coral is robust enough to sustain low to moderate tourism ventures."

"But you don't want people in the city?"

"No doubt some will venture into the city but I certainly don't wish to promote it. We don't have the infrastructure. But yes, controlled tours into the interior are a possibility— we have ancient ruins that will be of interest. But it's the diving you'll be interested in going to first, I imagine."

He imagined right. But this wasn't about her. This was about her sister. And her sister liked the glamorous life.

"I'd love to see everything the average reader of the magazine I write for is interested in. The long, white, sandy beaches, the glamour of the desert, Bedouin tents, that sort of thing…" She glanced at him from under her lashes, suddenly aware that her mind had drifted at the thought of a tent, and Razeen. She cleared her throat. "Got anywhere like that? Where a girl, not exactly wanting authentic culture, but an 'experience' might want to go?"

He frowned. "This isn't Disneyland, Lucy, nor Hollywood; it's not a sanitized version of Arabia."

"I know. But not every visitor will want 'authenticity'. They want a holiday in the sun with a bit of difference."

The frown disappeared. "You're correct, of course." He sat back, his fist rubbing his lips as he focused his dark eyes on her. The dappled shade of the overhead leaves made it hard to read his thoughts. But, given the long pause, and the slight upward tilt of his lips, they were no doubt along the same, errant lines, as hers. "There are places I can arrange to have you taken."

Her heart thudded in her chest. She didn't want a member of his staff showing her around. She needed him. She needed to be alert for a slip in his speech, she needed to learn of his needs and desires. She needed him. He was the key to finding Maia.

She hesitated only briefly before leaning toward him. "You said you wanted to get to know me, Razeen. What better opportunity than showing me your country?"

His face didn't change expression; he continued to stare at her. She willed herself not to blink, not to blush, not to reveal how much was riding on his answer. Then his face relaxed into a faint, tense smile.

"You're right, again." He didn't lean toward her. Hesitatingly, self consciously, Lucy sat back in her chair. She'd made an advance and it hadn't been accepted. "Meanwhile, I have work to complete. I'll take you back to your room and I'll have someone bring you to me later. I'll take you round Sitra this afternoon, if you wish?

"That would be great, thanks."

"Or perhaps you would like to rest? I believe you didn't get much sleep last night."

She grinned. "I'm used to it. I don't sleep well."

"Too many mid-night swims perhaps."

"That and too many vivid dreams."

"Me also." He held her gaze with an intensity of need that both scared and mesmerized her. The silence between them stretched too long to continue with polite conversation. He rose and extended his hand to hers. She accepted it and he pulled her to him. Slowly, so slowly he placed both his hands over hers and brought them to his lips. Such an old-fashioned gesture, yet the effect of the pressure of his lips against her skin was anything but tame. She pulsed deep inside, her body reacting to his touch like a slackly strung cello string played long and low: vibrating, in tune, shivering under his touch. She felt his touch long after his hands had left her. "Lucy Gee. Where did you come from?" His voice was gravelly with lust.

"From out of the blue."

"And is that where you'll disappear to?"

She nodded, trying to focus on his words when all she wanted to do was focus on his body. "I have two weeks before I return."

"Two weeks." He said slowly. "That's convenient. Come. I'll take you back to your room." He took her by the hand and led her out into brilliant sunshine.

Her body and mind were in turmoil. She couldn't deny the attraction that did more than simmer between them. Everything about him set her on fire: from the firm grip of his hand on hers, to the intensity of his gaze and the memory of last night's kiss. But this was the man whom Maia has fallen for, with whom she had been last seen. Was she going to follow in her sister's footsteps and be the next to disappear in this medieval foreign land?

With each step she took beside him, with each subtle shift and squeeze of his fingers against her skin, the answer became more certain. Yes, she was. Because her body couldn't deny him and because it was the only way to find Maia.

The return to her room was much quicker than the route she'd taken. At her door he halted, gave her hand a sweeping caress with his thumb before dropping it to her side. "I look forward to showing you around later."

"Do you always take such care of your employees?"

Again that smile. "No. Nor do I give them a bedroom suite so close to mine."

She fumbled with the door handle, suddenly unable to face him, or the fact that the blatant sexual vibe between them wasn't only on her side. He wanted her too. He was imagining them picking up where they'd left off, just as she was. Having the undercurrents suddenly thrust out into the open should have made her realize how impossible the situation was. But all she could think about was how close he was to her.

Before she could open the door, he'd slid his fingers under her chin and brought her lips to his. Her heart pounded once, twice, from lust and something else she refused to contemplate: the guilt could wait. He held his lips to hers, barely moving his mouth for seconds, as if he were testing her, rather than tasting her. Slowly she slipped under his spell, her eyelids flickering closed as her senses sunk under the power of his touch.

He withdrew leisurely, his narrowed eyes never leaving hers, as if assessing her response. "Until later, Lucy…" His thumb dragged lightly across her lips. And then he was gone: lost amidst the lush growth of the gardens.

She opened the door, rushed inside and fell back against the closed door, pressed her eyes shut with her fingers and cursed.

What the hell was she doing? Even if he wasn't implicated in Maia's disappearance, Lucy Gee didn't do relationships, she didn't do emotional intimacy. She just kept moving on to the next thing. Always moving. It wasn't only that it was part of the pact she'd made with Maia to experience everything. It was more than that. Lucy had no wish to repeat the devastation of her first love and its dire consequences. She refused to ever go there again, to risk herself again. And here she was playing with fire because without that fire, she couldn't find Maia.

CHAPTER FOUR

Lucy thanked the attendant who'd brought her back to Razeen's private gardens. She pushed the heavy bough of flowers back and walked out to the seating area that overlooked the bay. The unbroken line of the horizon melted into the intensely blue sky. The welcome sea breeze shifted the heavy air and Lucy relaxed within sight and sound of the sea once more. She didn't think she could live without having the sea close by. It had been a point of difference between Lucy and Maia: she needed the sea and Maia had always sought the crowded cities of Europe. So what the hell was Maia doing miles from anywhere?

If Maia was here, anywhere in Sitra, she'd be in the city. Lucy surveyed the jumble of buildings with their uneven roofs above which heat shimmered, distorting the chaos even further. It was all so physically close, and yet it felt as if it were a different world. Whether it was or not, she'd soon find out. Razeen had promised to show her the city. She turned away from the view, trailing her hand over the heavy blooms, releasing their sweet fragrance and a spray of water that showered her hand and arm in a momentary flash of rainbow colors.

"A rainmaker, hey?"

Lucy turned around sharply. Razeen was standing close by looking highly amused.

"I should have known," he continued. "The day you arrived in my country, a storm was forecast—it's due to arrive in a few days."

She grinned. "I've always thought of

myself as powerful, but not quite on the weather-making scale."

He walked over to her and she turned to face him, instinctively wanting her body to be close to his.

"You mustn't underestimate yourself. I can quite imagine you wield an influence far beyond your knowing."

Her smile faded as she looked into his eyes: eyes that had ceased to joke, but held a curious sadness she couldn't fathom.

"I think I'd prefer not to know the extent of any powers I may have. I may use them for evil. Ignorance is bliss and all that."

He cast her a quick sidewards glance. "Ignorance is never bliss. And that's why I asked you here. The afternoon is the best time to see the sights Sitra has to offer." He smiled, relaxed, once more. "I'd be pleased to show you around."

"Won't you being the King make that

a little difficult?"

"I will go incognito."

"Ah, hence the plain robes."

"Indeed."

"And hence only one bodyguard." She inclined her head toward the powerful-looking guard who was waiting for them at the top of some winding stone steps.

He grinned. "That is low-key for me, believe me."

"But surely you're safe in your own city?"

"Of course. Sometimes I think the guard is there to keep me from mixing with the people, rather than the other way round." Lucy frowned, struck by the wistful tone in his voice. "Let's go. Most people will be resting in an hour or so. Then, we will have the places we will visit to ourselves. It will be better that way."

Better for whom, Lucy thought as she followed him down the worn steps that clung precipitously to the outside wall of the palace before emerging onto the main street of Sitra. Being alone with Razeen wouldn't help her find Maia. And it might just end in her losing herself.

Out on the street, Lucy was hit by a wall of heat and noise. Stalls selling everything imaginable lined the roadside and there were people everywhere—the women in black, the men in white—surging around the pavement and the street. She recoiled momentarily before forcing herself to continue.

"Anything wrong?" Razeen stopped walking and drew her to him, under the shade of a faded awning.

She was surprised he'd noticed. It seemed he was as aware of her, as she was of him. "It's just so…"

"Chaotic?"

She nodded.

"That's what I enjoy most. But it's not threatening, you'll get used to it." He frowned. "But you do seem out of your element, like a mermaid washed ashore."

"A fish out of water. You're not far wrong."

"Do you wish to continue?"

Maia. The single word floated across her mind like a shadow. "Of course. I'd love to see everything about the city."

He frowned. "Are you sure?"

She smiled briefly, desperately trying to summon up the confidence that she usually felt but which was weakened here, now, with him. She smiled again. "Yes, I'm sure. Let's go and you can tell me what it was like growing up here."

They were soon part of the crowds. She was tense to begin with, watching the faces of passers-by to see if they singled her and Razeen out. But, with her tanned skin and dark glasses, no one gave her a second glance, and

Razeen's nondescript robes obviously achieved their aim of completing disguising the new King. Which was odd, she thought, given he was taller than most. Surely, even dressed in ordinary robes, people would still recognize him? Lucy was beginning to wonder if the average person knew anything about their King.

"I guess being the son of the King must have made life pretty easy for you?"

He shook his head. "It was almost as if I had two lives."

"Really?"

"Yes, within the palace I was the irritating youngest child who, more often than not, was in the way. It was extremely formal." He pursed his lips briefly. "My mother was...reclusive and my father and brother were very similar, and very close."

"Sounds suffocating."

"It was. That's why I used to escape."

"Where to? The sea? The hills?"

He laughed. "I am not you, Lucy. Despite what it may seem in the palace where my advisors insist on formality, on keeping my distance from everyone, I have always been drawn to people. I used to run off into the market and play with the boys there."

"Did they know who you were?"

"No," he laughed. "They had no idea. I was just another skinny boy with more interest in playing games, eating bread fresh from the pan and kissing girls, than studying the dry subjects my brother was interested in."

"Kissing girls came last on your list?" She teased.

He turned a narrowed gaze on her and her heart suddenly raced. "Always first."

She took a deep breath. "I can imagine."

He shifted closer to her. "Even at University, my interests stayed much the same."

"They do degrees in such things?"

He grinned. "I wish. No, my studies were fitted around my interests."

"You were very consistent, then." She licked her lips. "Your commitment to your interests didn't waver."

"If you want to be good at something, then you have to practice. If you want to be a connoisseur of something, you need to know it well."

She swallowed and dragged a breath deep into her lungs. "And did you succeed…in becoming a connoisseur?"

His lips curved into a sensual smile. "Now *that*, I'm hoping you will discover yourself." He searched her face and whatever he found there appeared to confirm his hopes and his smile deepened. "But for now, my bodyguard, Assad, is becoming impatient with our meandering. Come, I'll show you a few sights. Give you some background to your magazine article."

"What first?" She looked away from him, trying to concentrate on the reason she was here.

"The Great Mosque of Sitra. Look, over there, up on the hill facing the palace—the gold domes, the minarets—that's The Great Mosque. It's very old and revered by Christian and Muslim alike. It's very special." He turned back to her. "That is, if you'd like to see it. Perhaps, instead, you'd prefer a quiet afternoon at the palace." He cast a quick look around and, obviously satisfied they weren't overlooked, tucked a stray lock of hair back under her scarf. "I have given myself the afternoon off."

Her body screamed to accept his invitation. From the casual touch to her hair that blasted a heated trail deep inside of her, to the light in his eyes when he talked of the days of his childhood, he communicated a warmth

97

and ease that lay at the heart of his charm. But there was only one thing that stopped her. The old compass shifted stickily between her breasts under her robes. She had no bearings until she found Maia.

"The mosque, Razeen, please. I'd like to see the mosque and everything else the city has to offer."

He frowned, uncertainly. He probably wasn't used to his advances being rebuffed. But he soon recovered and turned to her with his usual charming smile.

"The mosque it is."

The mosque—with its central dome, its minarets, from which the muezzin gave the call to prayer, and the arcades, which ran parallel to the direction of prayer toward Mecca—was stunning. And it moved Lucy in a way she hadn't expected. Its exquisite decorations and sheer size was breathtaking. But the mosque, together with the places that Razeen took her to afterwards, did nothing to further her search for Maia.

However, she thought as she took off her sunglasses, there was one thing she'd learned. They were walking alongside the women's market and when she turned toward the market, her gaze was met by a dozen stares. Lucy's green eyes signaled her status as a *ferenji*, or foreigner. She'd learned that there were no other westerners here and she knew that there was no way the pale-skinned, red-haired Maia could be in the city without there being talk. And it was *that* talk that she needed to listen to. It should be easy enough. Razeen had commented that, despite his father's isolationist policies, many people in his country knew a little English, and some a lot, with the increased opportunities to study abroad and cable TV. If only she could persuade Razeen to let her enter the market alone.

She slipped her sunglasses back on and turned to Razeen.

"Can we stop here for a bit?"

"I'm sorry, I've been thoughtless. You need refreshment." Razeen signaled for a vendor to step forward with a glass of pomegranate juice and Lucy drank it thankfully.

"That was delicious, but I was wondering if we could enter the souk."

Razeen frowned. "It's the woman's market. I can't enter."

"But—"

"I can't let you go alone. Tomorrow, perhaps. I'll organize for some women to accompany you."

Lucy wracked her brain, trying to come up with a reason for her to go alone but before she could answer a palace official appeared and bowed before them.

"Your Majesty."

Irritated by the public address,

Razeen turned to the man with a scowl. "What is it?"

"Urgent business at the palace. Your senior advisor has requested you come immediately."

Razeen's face turned grim and he closed his eyes briefly as if trying to keep his irritation in check.

"I'm sorry, Lucy. I must leave you now but Assad will keep you company if you wish to look around further."

"That would be great. There's so much to see."

"I will see you later." His lips briefly curled into a smile but his eyes remained stern.

Razeen was soon lost amongst the crowds and Lucy wandered over to the women's market. She turned to see an irritated Assad—obviously unimpressed with his demotion to look after a foreign visitor, and a woman at that—checking his cell phone for messages. Lucy took her chance and slipped away into the depths of the women's market, where the guard wasn't able to follow.

It was late afternoon and the souk was teeming with people after the post-lunch Qaylulah during which they rested. Lucy wove her way through the narrow aisles between stalls laden with produce of every variety. But it was the food stalls that drew her. She'd always loved food; the alchemy of turning raw ingredients into something special fascinated her. She stopped beside a spice stall where bags brimmed with spices the color of the sun—red, pale yellow, deep gold, burnished orange—some familiar and some completely unknown to her.

The woman, whose stall it was, caught her eye and spoke to her in rapid Arabic. Lucy smiled and shook her head. She dipped her head to smell a brilliant orange spice. Again the woman tried to speak to her and again, she shook her head. This time, however, the woman spoke to another much younger woman who had her back to them. She turned around and eyed Lucy directly.

"English?"

Surprised, Lucy nodded. "I'm from New Zealand. Do you speak English?"

"Yes. My friend's brother lives in the US and sends her TV shows. I borrow them and we both learn English. My friend's brother says I am good."

"You are."

The young woman smiled shyly. "My name is Aakifah."

"And mine, Lucy."

"L'see?"

Lucy grinned. "Yes."

The other woman poured forth a stream of Arabic to Aakifah. "My mother asks if you buy her spices or just smell them?"

Lucy grinned at the mother. "I'd love to buy some but I don't recognize them

all and I'm not sure how they're used.
Could your mother tell me?"

Aakifah turned to her mother and they
had an animated conversation. "My
mother says she will show you." She
turned and spoke rapidly to yet another
young woman. "My sister will work the
stall."

"Great!" Lucy plucked off her
sunglasses and followed Aakifah round
the back of the roughly-built stall.
"Thank you," she smiled and nodded
to the older woman who was already
squatting beside a small stove, heating
oil in a shallow pan.

She was soon on her haunches
beside the other women, listening to
Aakifah's translations of her mother's
descriptions of the spices and the meat
and grains with which she used them.
Soon, other women were grouped
around them having heard that there
was a *ferenji* in the market. Before long
the old woman had served up a plate of

food and urged Lucy to taste it.

Lucy took a mouthful, closed her eyes and sighed. "Fantastic!" She gestured her approval to the older woman who grinned widely.

"My mother asks that you show us what cooking you do, please."

"I'd love to."

Lucy bought a selection of ingredients with Aakifah's help and before long she was cooking a dish that had long been a favorite amongst the crews of the boats she'd worked on.

Spoonfuls were handed around to an appreciative audience.

"Mother said this is very good indeed. She especially likes the way you've used the lemon with the spices. But she wonders if your husband and children are accepting of the lack of goat meat."

Lucy paused for a long moment suddenly aware of the wide gulf that divided them. "I have no husband or children."

After Aakifah translated, there was a collective gasp and a murmur of disbelief rippled around the group.

"It's normal in the West not to marry until you're older," Lucy continued, feeling a need to justify the behavior the others obviously saw as very strange. "Western women like to pursue a career, live an independent life."

There was much shaking of heads and pitying looks.

"Mother says that it is a waste of beauty and skill to be a spinster."

"Thank your mother for her compliments but please assure her I'm perfectly happy as I am." Met with disbelieving looks, Lucy suddenly felt uncomfortable. She'd spent enough time in the souk. She needed to get back to the palace and she still hadn't asked the question she needed to know the answer to. "I am looking for someone, Aakifah—my sister. I think she may be in Sitra. Do you see many westerners here? Have you heard of a very beautiful woman, tall, red hair, very pale skin?"

Aakifah frowned and spoke briefly to the small crowd who'd gathered around them. There was a jumble of worried responses but the plethora of shaking heads made Lucy's heart sink. "If your sister is in Sitra she has not been through the city. We would have heard of such a person. She sounds like a *jinn*, a ghost."

Lucy forced a disappointed smile to her face and stood up. "She's no ghost. Perhaps, as you say, she's not even here. Anyway, I have to go now. Please thank your mother. It's been great. Very kind. Very hospitable."

The old woman obviously understood the meaning and nodded enthusiastically while talking in a stream of Arabic to her daughter. "She says you must come again."

"I'd love to."

Aakifah walked with Lucy to the edge of the market where they both stopped. As Lucy scanned the crowds for the guard, she was aware Aakifah was studying her, her eyebrows drawn together in a puzzled frown. "Where you stay in Sitra, L'cee?"

"At the palace. The person I worked for knows the King who has allowed me to stay there for a few weeks."

Aakifah's eyes widened. "The new King? You are very honored. But," the woman bit her lip and glanced up under long dark lashes, "aren't you frightened?"

Lucy frowned. "Frightened? Why should I be?"

"The new King is very stern. He makes big changes in our land. The elders believe his ways are too foreign; they do not like what he is doing."

"But things have improved, haven't they? There seems no shortage of food in the markets."

"That is true. It is not like before. The poor people have more money, more food. Life is not so hard."

"Then I think the fears of the elders must be that they're losing their money to the poor."

Aakifah's brief look of shock turned to laughter as she embraced Lucy and they parted. "I hope you will visit us again, L'cee."

"I hope so too."

"Goodbye L'cee."

The last syllable followed Lucy out into the street as if calling out to the sea that she so loved.

After an initial barrage of unintelligible Arabic, Lucy had to endure a stony silence from Assad until he deposited her inside the palace gates, leaving her with a cursory bow. With no idea how to retrace her steps to her room, Lucy wandered toward the main offices where she was directed to wait in the public reception rooms where the King had granted a public audience to some people embroiled in a land dispute. Lucy thought it appeared medieval somehow that people were allowed to sit in on meetings but she went and sat on the seats arranged at the rear of the room.

There was only a handful of people there watching. What struck her was the distance between Razeen and the people to whom he was listening. She thought he'd get up at any moment to bridge the gap that so obviously existed, not just physically but in the tone of the people. But he didn't. Razeen looked so alone up there. Why didn't people sit with him? Why weren't the people talking to him made to feel comfortable, at ease? He appeared a different man to the one she was getting to know. There was no humor, no approachability, no sense that he was listening to the people. And he was, she was sure of it. Only it didn't look as though he was. She slipped outside and waited for Razeen to finish.

At last the people drifted away through the public entrance and Razeen stepped outside the rear door with his ministers. He caught sight of Lucy sitting under the shade of a tree and came toward her. She jumped up, her heart racing at the sight of him, and smiled in response to the flare of heat in his eyes.

"I hear you gave Assad the slip. He wasn't impressed with your vanishing act."

He drew his arm around her and they walked up through the sprawling palace.

"I wanted to go to the women's market and, well, he couldn't come too, could he? One of the women found him and told him what I was doing. He knew

I was safe. What did he think would happen to me there?"

"You'd be surprised. An unauthorized foreign visitor arrived some years ago and was stoned by the women."

Lucy was shocked. "I can't believe it. Those women were just wonderful, they wouldn't do something like that."

"They're good women. But they're also traditional women. They don't like strangers coming into their world wearing clothes that are distasteful to them. It threatens everything they live their lives by. It frightens them. And frightened people are dangerous people."

"Well, they appear to accept me okay. I guess the abaya and hijab helped."

"So what did you do there?"

"Cooked."

He raised his an eyebrow. "Now *that*, I hadn't imagined."

"They showed me how to make chicken kabsa and khubz and I showed them how to make spicy bean fritters with a yummy lemon sauce."

"You must have made an impression on them."

"And they, on me."

He frowned and turned to her, searching her eyes for an answer as if her answer was of the utmost importance to him. "Good or bad?"

She paused briefly. "Beyond good. I hadn't imagined they would be so wonderfully welcoming, so interesting and so…"

He looked away as if confused by her answer. "Different? They must have thought your behavior very strange, for someone staying at the palace."

"They did. And I didn't understand why. But I'm beginning to." She searched his face, wondering if he would answer the question she was dying to ask him. It was personal but he'd ceased to be the King. She could only think of him as Razeen: the man who loved people but who was forced to keep his distance, the man who was doing a job he'd not been raised or educated for. "Why are you so distant with people?"

"Distant?" Any sense of outrage at her personal question was quickly contained. "It's just the way it is; the way it's always been. If I were more familiar, the people wouldn't like it. Our culture is very different to your own, Lucy. You mustn't forget that."

She opened her mouth to disagree but had second thoughts. As she gazed out at the tumble of roofs of the city buildings below the palace, she no longer saw inanimate objects, but imagined the people beneath them: living, breathing people with desires and interests like her own. They *were* different, yet not so very much. "Perhaps, in some ways. But in others, they're very similar. I guess people are people anywhere. One thing with my business, people have to eat. It's the same the world over. Wherever I go I connect with people over food."

They'd reached her door. "Speaking of which, will you join me for dinner? Just us." He added as if reading her mind.

She needed an opportunity to discover if he knew anything about Maia. If, as she was beginning to think, Maia wasn't in Sitra and he knew nothing of her whereabouts, then she could enjoy herself. As her suspicions had lessened during the day, so, too, had her defenses against her attraction to Razeen. The reasons for keeping her distance were diminishing by the hour. But until her suspicions were completely proved false, she *had* to keep a barrier between them.

"Couldn't think of anything I'd rather do."

"Good. Until later, then." He touched her cheek in a gentle, yet intimate farewell and turned to walk away.

"Where shall I go?" She called after him.

"I'll come for you at seven." He turned and grinned. "And bring a bikini."

CHAPTER FIVE

The fiery ball of the sun dipped below the horizon and dusk fell like a curtain bringing sudden darkness to the city, leaving Lucy with a heightened sense of anticipation for the night ahead.

She glanced down at the loose trousers and shirt she wore and for the hundredth time and hoped they'd be suitable. Razeen had assured her she could wear what she wished tonight, that they wouldn't be going anywhere too public. The thought had both reassured and thrilled her. And the deep thrumming thrill had only intensified as she'd waited for him to arrive.

Right on time, there was a knock at the door. Lucy sucked in a long, slow breath, willing herself to be calm as she answered it. The air rushed right out again at the sight of Razeen, his tall, strong body clad not in robes, but in casual trousers and open-necked shirt that revealed just how toned his body was. He stood, one hand leaning against the wall, his gaze focused on the ancient tiles at his feet as if deep in thought. His shirt sleeves were rolled up revealing muscled forearms and his chest… It was all she could do not to spread her fingers out over that chest and feel the friction of the sprinkling of hairs against her skin. When he lifted his eyes to hers, the contemplative look was swiftly replaced by a devastating heat that reflected her own.

"Miss Gee. Are you ready?"

She nodded, unable to stop her heart skipping out of time at the sight and scent of him. Without his keffiyeh

Lucy could see his hair was shortish, but long enough to run her fingers through. His cheekbones were broad and his lips were habitually pressed firmly together, as if determined to show restraint. Despite the control, the intensely sensual look in his narrowed eyes as they met hers, showed his true thoughts.

"Absolutely. Do I need an abaya?"

The silence lengthened as he looked her up and down appreciatively. "You are perfect, exactly as you are."

"It's just that I wouldn't want to offend anyone, I, well…" Lucy trailed off, embarrassed by the compliment, evident not only in his words, but also in his eyes.

"I can assure you, you do not offend me, quite the reverse. Shall we go?" She took his offered arm gratefully and he squeezed it against his body in a momentary, subtle embrace designed to reassure.

"Sure." She tried to keep focused, but walking closely beside Razeen, inhaling his personal scent, would have destroyed the concentration of a Zen master. "So," she gulped another lungful of Razeen-laden air, "where exactly are we going?"

"Back where we first met, the next bay along to be exact. We'll dine there. My family has a lodge there. I'm thinking of using it as a model for the first phase of tourism. I'd like your opinion of it."

A flutter of anticipation ran through Lucy. It had nothing to do with Maia and all to do with the thought of an evening alone with Razeen.

"Sounds good." Too good. She needed him; but she also needed to keep her distance and her head.

Instead of walking through the palace down to the city, Razeen took her through secret gardens surrounded by high walls: ancient enclosures, far bigger than the courtyards and gardens elsewhere within the palace, where columns, that appeared to be Roman, still upheld stone pergola. They followed the lie of the land down from the crest of the hill through lush greenery until they came to a large door that Razeen unbolted. He nodded in greeting to the guards in the guardhouse beside the door and then they walked on, down the long flight of ancient steps to a small private bay. The bay was empty except for a large, modern boathouse. Ignoring the huge motor launch Razeen guided Lucy to a small motorboat. He pressed a button on the large doors which slid back revealing the inky blue water and night sky.

"Quite a contrast: state of the art boat shed next to Roman ruins."

"I need my escape to be secure." He grinned and her stomach tied into knots.

He stepped into the boat and held out his hand to her. She jumped into his arms and he brought her softly towards his body, his hands slipping gently around her waist. His white shirt gleamed in the darkened boathouse. She dropped her head and drew in a deep breath, infused with the warm notes of leather and ambergris. There was no sound except their quickened breathing and the gentle lap of the water against the rear of the shed.

Her gaze dropped to his lips, which parted in response. She swayed, suddenly disoriented and he tightened his grip on her, as if aware of her slightest movement. He held her for a moment before running his hand down the side of her body from her ribs to her hips, sending a rush of sensation down the length of her.

"I'm glad you are not wearing an abaya tonight."

"As you'd mentioned a bikini, I

imagined we weren't going anywhere formal."

"You're right. We're less formal within the private quarters of the palace and where we're going. I think you will find us less savage, more sophisticated than you can imagine."

"I have a vivid imagination."

He eyes narrowed as if he were trying to contain a secret thought. "Good. I'll make sure we put it to good use."

Lucy could feel the flush rising from deep inside. His hot gaze stripped her of the clothing as if it wasn't there. She felt as naked as if she'd worn only the bikini. She wanted to pull away—he was too dangerous—but she needed him; she needed him to let down his guard and tell her where her sister was. She swallowed.

"In what way?"

He drew closer to her again so that she could feel the heat from his body, the subtle friction of his shirt against her skin, his breath against her cheek. She couldn't keep her eyes off his lips. They were almost stern lips, but she knew the effect they could have on her. He dipped his head, his nose brushing her cheek; his lips tantalizingly close to hers. All thoughts of distance fled and instinctively she shifted her head in a soft angle so that he could kiss her. But the kiss didn't come and, instead, she watched the mouth she wanted so much to touch hers, curve into a delicious smile and withdraw from her.

"I can think of many ways. However," he smiled further and pulled away suddenly, "there's no hurry. We are alone here, with the sea and the stars. We have all the time in the world."

She pulled away in confusion as the needs of her body clashed with the thoughts that whirled in her brain. She sat at the front of the boat, as Razeen turned on the engine. Within minutes they'd slid out into the inky sea. The deep-throated roar of the boat broke the silence. As they sped out of the secluded bay into the darkening ocean, she was once more overwhelmed by the beauty of the place. Behind them the palace gardens sprawled over the ridge, only a string of gleaming lights penetrated the leafy darkness to indicate the path they'd followed. To her right the city suddenly came into sight. There were no flashing neons, only pale twinkling lights emerged from the dun-colored houses. Nor was there a halo of bright light crowning the city to obscure the stars that were beginning to emerge in the dense indigo sky. The darkness of the city allowed the stars to reveal their full glory.

They sped past the city, skirting the harbor with its tangle of white sails that gleamed dully in the dusk. Sitting in the bow of the boat, Lucy welcomed the opportunity to hide behind her wind-whipped hair. The soft spray fell upon her skin and she breathed deeply of the warm, damp air. She always felt most relaxed when she was at sea but tonight—caught between her attraction to Razeen and her fears for Maia—she felt emotional. She rarely cried but now tears pricked her eyes and she shivered. Must be the quickened wind, she thought as she surreptitiously swiped her fingers under her eyes.

As the boat turned its back to the wind and began to return to shore, she closed her eyes for a few moments willing the confusion of emotions to subside. She was here to find her sister; instead she'd found a man whose very touch made her forget everything that was important to her. She *had* to pull herself together, forget the things that threatened her purpose. She couldn't go to pieces now; she'd come too far.

Razeen slowed the boat as a jetty

came into view. There appeared nothing beyond it. She couldn't see anything but flat sand dunes. But as they came closer a dark shape loomed to the right of them, only slightly higher than the surrounding land. Razeen carefully maneuvered the boat until it was alongside the jetty, cut the engine, expertly threw out a rope around a post and jumped out. He offered his hand but she didn't take it immediately. She turned back a moment to gaze out at the inky sea, almost loathe to leave its anonymity behind, scared, for the first time in a long time, to face what lay on shore.

"Lucy?"

His eyes were bright in the dusky light. They narrowed as he tried to work out the reason for her hesitance.

"Yes, sorry." She took his hand and he helped her onto the jetty but then he withdrew his hand as if aware of her doubts.

"Is everything all right?"

She tried to smile, but her mouth felt tight with apprehension. What the hell was she doing? She knew what happened when she let her emotional defenses down. She'd been there and done that at fifteen and she didn't plan to ever be that emotionally vulnerable again. Since then she'd always protected herself, always been in control. But now she felt as if she were a piece of wood, floating on the sea, at the mercy of the tides. And the tides had chosen to wash her up on this shore, with this man, from whom just one touch left her feeling exposed.

"Sure." She forced herself to relax. They fell into step, their footsteps sounding hollow on the jetty, beneath which the sea surged.

"So what's on your mind— what's giving you such a pensive expression?"

"Memories, that's all." Not a complete

lie.

"But you've not been here before."

"No. It's all so strange and so beautiful but it still reminds me of home in an odd way."

"And where is home?"

"The New Zealand coast—unspoiled, wide, expansive."

"I've never been there. I hear it's beautiful." He paused. "How often do you return?"

"Never," she shrugged. "There's nothing there for me now. I haven't been back in eight years, since I was sixteen."

He frowned. "You have no family to visit?"

The smile trembled on her lips. "They're scattered around the globe."

"And that doesn't worry you? You don't wish to settle down?"

Was it Lucy's imagination or did she sense the question was important behind its cloak of politeness?

"No. I don't want to settle, ever. I love traveling and I love the sea so my job is perfect."

He'd come to a halt and he nodded his head, as if the answer pleased him. "This way." He brushed her arm lightly and she closed her eyes in the darkness as his touch flitted softly through her body, opening up her feelings in a way she hadn't experienced for so long and quieting those fears his touch should have ignited.

As his hand slid down her arm, he took her hand in his and they walked up to the house. It was only when they stood in front of it that she realized what she'd thought was the sky, was a wall of glass. The lodge was long and low, its entire front was made of glass that reflected and merged with the sky. Further dwellings were clustered some distance from the lodge. A sensor light clicked on and light rained out onto the grasses, lending them a curious silver quality, draining all color.

He slid back the doors to reveal a room furnished simply with oversized sofas set on a dark-stained wooden floor. One wall was covered in books. He turned on some music and speakers softly came into life.

"Is this your retreat from the world?" She walked up to the books, drawn to the vast array, and trailed her fingertips gently over them. "So many books."

"I have little time for reading at the palace. I come here to rest, to relax. Do you enjoy reading?"

She frowned and shook her head. "Never got into the habit."

"But at school?"

"Nah. I didn't hang about at school." She fixed a bright smile on her face— only her sister knew the real reason she'd left school so young— and turned to him. "I wanted to get out, see the world, live a little."

He showed her through to the dining room where dinner was laid out for them. "And your family didn't mind?"

"My mother died when I was twelve and my father was long gone." She shrugged. "Went off with another woman."

"I'm sorry."

She glanced up sharply, the old defensiveness springing back into life again. "Why? I'm not. It made me stand on my own two feet; it made me realize no one else was going to make my life for me, except me."

"Sounds lonely."

She turned away to look out over the sea. "I have my sister."

"You're still close to her?"

She sat very still, aware of him seating himself opposite, but focused on the soft drawing of the sea on the sand outside their window. "Yes." She forced herself to look into his eyes. "Yes," she repeated, stronger now.

"She cared for me after mum died. She was only sixteen but she worked as model, waitress, whatever, so she could keep me at school, keep me with her."

"And the authorities let her?"

"They didn't know. It's easier to get lost in a system than one thinks."

"And your father, he didn't return when your mother died?"

"Dad came back but my sister sent him away again."

"Your sister sounds a formidable character, much like yourself."

"She is." Lucy frowned. "Generally, she is. I guess we all have our weaknesses."

"And hers is?"

"Glamor. She loves the high life. A reaction to her upbringing I guess. She's easily seduced by a smooth word here, a promise there, easily lulled by luxurious clothes, good food, parties, the high life."

"And you're not?"

"No." She held his gaze. "I don't trust any of those things."

"I sense you don't give your trust easily."

She shook her head, not willing to answer, not willing to elaborate on the source of her lack of trust.

"Me neither," he continued. "But I trust you."

She eyes widened in surprise. "Why?"

"Because you are, as you are. You don't pretend. There is nothing you need from me, nothing you need me to believe about yourself in order for me to give it."

Lucy's composure faltered only momentarily. "Tell me about yourself."

"Me?" He sighed. "I'm far less interesting than you."

"Yeah, right. You're a King and I'm a chef."

"Ah, but I was not groomed to be King. I was the younger son. My father believed I was better suited to the life of an English gentleman without responsibilities, or duties."

"Better suited?"

"Put it this way, my elder brother was much like my father. Both were traditionalists, both autocratic and an integral part of the elite of Sitra. I was not like them. I remember, when I was young, before I was sent to boarding school in England, questioning why something was done in a certain way. Neither my father nor my brother could explain, neither could see why an explanation was necessary. I was sent away shortly afterwards to Eton. I was not to be trusted with the tradition of Sitra."

"Perhaps your father wanted something different for you?"

"Thank you for your generous interpretation. But no, I wasn't well liked by my father, too curious, too wanting to challenge. Apparently not good traits in a leader."

"And yet here you are, leader to your country."

"My father died several years ago and brother died suddenly after a short illness last year. There was no one else, apart from the Kings of neighboring countries—Qawaran and Ma'in."

"Would they have tried to take over the country?"

Razeen laughed and shook his head. "No. They are our allies. Sitra has a treaty with both Qawaran, a mountainous region ruled by King Zahir and Ma'in, an important city state ruled by King Tariq. The three of us are strong together. Without one part of the three functioning, our lands would be vulnerable. I had no choice but to return."

"So you had to turn your back on your old life. That must have been hard."

He didn't answer immediately but she

saw the memories flit across his eyes like clouds casting shadows. "It should have been hard but it wasn't. A man can live only so long without real work. I was tired of a life that revolved around purely pleasure. There's nothing noble in that."

Lucy realized he was turning out to be quite a different character to the one she'd first imagined.

"I don't know," she tried to keep it light. "That's what I aim to do. Keep on moving, keep on enjoying life."

He poured out two glasses of champagne, handed her a glass and held up his own to hers. "To Lucy, may you one day find a place where you'll want to stay."

She shook her head nervously, as his words hit home with more precision than he could possibly have imagined. She took a sip of the dry, effervescent wine and swallowed hard. She shook her head more vigorously than she needed to, as if to convince herself as much as him. "Traveling suits me. I've no desire to stay in one place. Ever."

He frowned. "What are you running from?"

She held his gaze, unable to bring a smile to her lips to reassure him, as the sharp stab of painful memories threatened to emerge. She shook her head again. "Nothing." And with that one negative word, the memories receded. "Traveling just suits me, that's all."

His frowned deepened as if he didn't accept her answer. "What made you want to come to Sitra? You sought out Alex's boat and you sought out my country. Why?"

Her heartbeat quickened and she took another studied drink of champagne, buying time for her voice to steady. "I've told you. Do you think so little of your country to imagine I wouldn't want to come here?"

"Not at all. But I do know my country is little known outside its immediate environs. I'm curious."

She placed the glass on the table with slow deliberation. "I'm sure you've shown other westerners around, other people, women perhaps?"

"A few."

Her heart was thumping. "What was it that intrigued them, what was it they wanted to see?"

"Not the night life, that's for sure. My friends—some of them—wished to see the country I'd inherited: its history, the beauty of the shore and the natural wonders, such as the city of caves."

"City of caves. I've not heard of that."

"In the interior is a mountainous area where the rock has formed natural caves. These caves have been excavated over millennia to provide homes for the Bedouin."

"Sounds pretty basic."

"Not so basic as you might imagine.

I'll take you there if you're interested."

"Definitely. The magazine I contribute to is always on the look-out for unique articles."

"I'll make arrangements this week to take you."

"Can you afford the time off?"

"As it happens, the next week or so is the last chance I have for some holiday. I'm fully committed after that."

"Good timing, then."

He lifted his glass. "Here's to good timing."

She raised her glass to his, the light catching the cut glass and showering it all around them. "May it bring us both what we want." And Lucy could see exactly what Razeen wanted by the way his eyes darkened with desire.

He raised his glass. "To mutual satisfaction." He lightly clinked his glass against hers. "Later, I will show you the attractions the Lodge offers after dark. But, for now, let's eat."

"Attractions after dark?" She raised an eyebrow. "That sounds…intriguing."

His lips quirked in an ambiguous smile. "I don't think I'll tell you yet. I'll let you dwell on it over dinner. But I'll give you a hint—it's a hobby of mine."

Lucy blinked, confused. "I can't say that reassures me."

He grinned. "Perhaps I don't wish you to be reassured, or comfortable."

Lucy didn't know if it was the way he was looking at her, or the alcohol she'd drunk, but her whole body felt alive with anticipation.

"Well, you're succeeding in that."

"Good, now eat."

"You know? Of all the things that had crossed my mind, this wasn't one of them."

Razeen laughed behind her as he slipped a hand on her shoulder and tilted the large telescope a little to the right.

"There, you will see a group of three stars—the Cyclades—they are the brightest they've been for twenty-five years. The interior and coastal area of Sitra are renowned for their dark skies and the brilliance of the stars."

Lucy put her eye to the telescope and the stars came into sharp focus. "The detail is amazing." She drew in a sharp breath as his hand covered hers in a brief caress before tilting it slightly in another direction.

"And that's Venus, the brightest star in the evening. It was recently in transit over the moon. An amazing sight."

Lucy didn't say anything but she continued to look at the planet, whose terrain she felt she could reach out and touch. It was something so far away, something so distant from her, so unreachable and yet there it was, a pale gold, shimmering under the slight quiver of light and movement that lay between her and it.

"It's beautiful, isn't it?"

She pulled away from the telescope suddenly, turned from Razeen and gazed up at the three-quarters moon, so bright, even though it wasn't yet full. "It's the most beautiful thing I've ever seen." She cleared her throat, which suddenly sounded hoarse. The dark water shifted silently below them, the night breeze rustled the palm fronds. Lucy willed the warm night air to cool her heated cheeks. When she'd collected herself, she turned to face him. He'd moved and was leaning with his back to the wooden railings, arms crossed, watching her.

The light of the stars and moon highlighted his cheeks and the whites of his eyes but his dark clothing and skin made him seem not himself. For a moment she could forget he was the last person she knew who had seen her sister. He was just himself—as beguiling, as seductive as the stars.

"*You*, Lucy, are a most unusual woman."

"No, I'm not."

He reached out and swept a strand of hair back away from her face and traced a finger down her cheek, his expression concentrated, as if trying to work her out from the line of her face.

She closed her eyes, desperately trying to repress her response to his touch.

"So beautiful, so fiercely independent, so fearless. You're like a wild bird soaring on the trade winds, being taken wherever the winds, or tides in your case, carry you. And now you've landed on my shore, I'd like to capture you for a short while."

His face was so close to hers that she couldn't see his features clearly. "Then you'd let me go?"

He smiled, his eyes crinkling up at the corners. "What a strange question. Do you think I'm in the habit of luring women to my palace, capturing them and never letting them go?"

He dropped his hand and walked back to the pool of light spilling out from the candlelit interior. His shape, form and details came into focus and Lucy saw him as the King once more. "I, I don't know." She twisted around uncomfortably before turning back to him again, nervously shrugging her shoulders.

He frowned suddenly and heavily, all humor gone. "No, Lucy, I'm not. You are the first woman I've brought to the Lodge. Since I've been in Sitra, I've not had a moment to myself. And that will continue. This time is a brief respite for me. Believe me."

Relief surged through her and she dropped her gaze, focusing on the track her toe was making through the layer of fine sand that covered the deck. "I do believe you."

God help her, she did. Whatever Maia

had done, wherever she was, it wasn't with Razeen. Suspicion slid from her mind like a weight and in its place her attraction bloomed loud and heavy. She walked over to him and he reached out for her hand and pulled her hard against him.

She gasped against his mouth as he first kissed her top lip, then her bottom lip, then touched the tip of her tongue with his. He groaned and slid his hands down and around her body, drawing her closer to him.

Part of her wanted to pull back, away from him. Not because she suspected him of being involved with Maia any longer, but because she'd never felt so attracted to a person before. It drew something from her that she always kept hidden. It felt new and dangerous. She wanted to travel the world light, she never wanted to leave anything behind. She never wanted to make herself vulnerable, like her mother had, like she herself had done once. But her body had other thoughts and she slipped her hands around his waist, her fingers finding and caressing the tight contours of his back and drawing him closer to her. The kiss deepened and when they eventually pulled apart, his mouth found her neck and she arched back, allowing the light of the moon to filter through her closed eyelids as she sank into sensation.

He slipped his hands to her bottom and caressed it before he pulled away. He rested his forehead against hers. "Lucy. Tell me if I am going to fast for you because if I had my way I would have you here and now. I seem to forget the finer points of seduction when I'm with you."

"Razeen." She moved her thumb against his lips and he closed his eyes as his mouth drew her thumb inside. A tremor of wanting shivered through her body and settled low. She smiled.

"Perhaps that's something I can teach you."

CHAPTER SIX

"We have all night, Razeen. And,"
she grinned, filled with relief that her
suspicions had proved groundless.
"You promised me a swim." She
glanced at her loose shirt. "I have
my bikini on underneath. I came
prepared." She watched him look down
at the bikini that was just visible at the
neckline and felt her nipples harden
under his scrutiny.

"So you did."

"Did *you*?"

"I'm always prepared."

She walked toward the steps, cast
a quick, teasing, glance behind her
to see his eyes hadn't left hers and

then jumped onto the sand. "Prepared enough for a race?"

She heard him follow and her walk turned into a jog, that turned into a run as she heard him just a few paces behind her. At the water's edge she quickly pulled off her clothes and ran into the sea until it was deep enough to dive into.

She turned, laughing, in time to see him toss his shirt on top of his trousers. Wearing only his shorts he dived into the sea and struck out strongly after her. She turned and continued to swim out to the pontoon that lay hardly moving in the mid-point of the bay. She'd only just placed her hands on the side of it when Razeen's arm wrapped around her waist and pulled her away, dumping her back in the sea while he hauled himself up.

"I'd say I won that race."

She laughed as she trod water. "I'd say you cheated."

"I think calling the King a 'cheat' is a punishable offense."

She swam up to the pontoon, placed her feet either side of his and quickly grabbed his ankles and pushed herself away from the side, pulling him into the water and submerging him. Laughing, she swam out of arm's reach. "And what's the offense for offending a King's dignity?"

"I'll show you when I get hold of you."

She twisted around and swam along the column of moonlight, out deeper into the ocean. But within two strokes she was pulled up by his hands around her legs. He pulled her firmly toward him and she suddenly slammed back into his body. His lips were on her neck and his arms around her waist as he supported her by treading water. His erection was hard against her bottom and back and she moved against it with each rise and fall of the gentle waves.

Suddenly he brought her around

and claimed her mouth with his own and she could do nothing but submit to his lips and his tongue. All rational thought fled; there was nothing but their two bodies in the element she'd always thought of as her own—water. She wrapped her legs around his hips and slammed intimately against him. His erection rubbing against her, hard and strong. She slid her arms around his neck, needing to deepen the kiss. The slight swell of the tide shifted their bodies, one against the other.

She pulled away and swam back to the pontoon where she hauled herself up onto its surface. He positioned himself between her legs and pushed himself up and kissed her nipples, one after the other, over the thin fabric of the bikini. She gasped and threw her head back, allowing him easier access to the nipples that ached to be touched. With a swift movement behind her he undid the tie that held her bikini top together and it fell away. He cupped her breasts and licked each one lazily. Deep inside her muscles clenched with pleasure, and moistened; her mind was drowsy with lust. He suckled her breasts, elongating the nipple, before raising his head to hers. She slipped forward so her sex met his on the side of the pontoon.

With another swift movement, he'd slipped off her bikini bottoms, dropped lower into the water and kissed her intimately. She fell back onto the pontoon and he slipped his hands under her bottom and pulled her to his mouth, the weathered wood abrading the sensitive skin of her back. White fire shot through her mind as his hard tongue moved upon her with precision, with regular thrusting movements, that sent her reeling over the edge. She cried out loud into the blank night and opened her eyes suddenly to see the stars, like a blanket above them both, silent witnesses to the all-consuming sensations that still surged and retreated within her.

Floating on the pontoon in the middle of the ocean, her body shot through with both sensation and satiation, she had the curious feeling she was floating, not on water, but on air, that she was disembodied and yet more alive than she'd ever felt before. She sat up and caressed his shoulders, her legs wrapping around his body as she slipped slowly back into the water, back around him.

"Lucy. You drive me crazy with need. But I can't be prepared in the middle of the ocean. Come with me to the beach where I can make love to you properly."

She kissed him long and hard. Then she fell away from him and floated on her back for a few seconds while he watched her—naked, her body white under the pale moonlight. Then she turned, flicked her feet and splashed him. He made a grab for her feet but she laughed and swam away.

"Race you back to shore."

"And you, Lucy, will win because your arousal doesn't curtail your movements."

But he was wrong. She didn't want to win. She kicked only enough to be slightly ahead of him and when he grabbed her foot toward him she didn't pull away. And when the water became shallow and he brought her to him and kissed her again, she didn't pull away. It was Razeen who eventually pulled away. He walked up to his clothes, extracted a package and returned to her, still lying in the shallows. He took off his shorts and threw them to land with the rest of his things. She ran her hand up his leg, along his silky length and cupped the weight of him in her hands. He groaned, rolled on the condom and dropped down on top of her. She wrapped her body around him with abandon and he slid into her immediately and held himself there, looking deep into her eyes.

"Razeen?" Her voice was hesitant.

He smoothed back the hair that lay plastered wetly across her face. "You are so beautiful, Lucy. So beautiful."

She shook her head and was about to deny her comment when he slipped out and pushed into her fiercely, drowning out any rational thought. The gentle surf pooled around her and the sand shifted beneath her body as he sank himself repeatedly into her. She curled her legs around him and drove her heels into his bottom, urging him into her, harder and faster. They came together and she fell back, her hair trailing on the surface of the waves.

Despite the barrage of sensations— of the water, and of him inside her— she was still aware of his breath, hot against her cheek, his lips gently tasting her as if he couldn't get enough of her, and his body deep inside hers, shifting slightly, setting her aflame with renewed desire.

They rolled onto their sides, still connected and kissed once more, but tenderly this time. He pulled away as if to see her but she curled her head against his chest. For some reason she couldn't name, she didn't want him to see her. Giving herself physically was one thing, but emotionally she'd always held herself in reserve. Razeen had blasted through that barrier and she felt more naked than she'd ever felt in her life.

"Lucy, what is it?"

She shivered slightly. "Nothing"

"You're cold? Come." He withdrew from her and stood up, reaching out his hand to hers. "I'll warm you in a hot shower."

He pulled her to his side and they walked naked up to the lodge, leaving their clothes behind. Droplets of water ran from his hair, down his body in slim rivulets that shone in the moonlight, before catching in the hair that tapered down from his stomach. Lucy pressed her fingers against his tight stomach, smiling to herself as the muscles clenched under her touch.

He smelled divine, too: of salt and of the night air. Her hand smoothed over his hips and caught the underside of his behind, her fingers curling under his bottom, as he walked. Aroused once more, she brought her other hand to the front and smoothed her hand down his semi-erect length. He growled, caught her hand and quickened his step until she had to run to keep up with him as they entered the Lodge.

As soon as they'd stepped inside he turned and kissed her fiercely, pressing his aroused body against hers. Too soon, he drew away and pulled her into the bathroom. He flicked the huge wet-room shower on full blast and

Lucy gasped as the hot water hit her body. The gasp was taken from her mouth as he pressed his lips against hers. Then he moved his lips down her body, pressing scorching hot kisses against her skin, hotter than the water that poured over them both. His mouth descended to her nipples, suckling them long and hard, making her cry out and fall back against the cold, tiled walls, her arms and hands splayed out on either side of her, seeking balance as she closed her eyes and water poured over her hair, face and body.

She was drowning in sensation as the suckling intensified and coils of tightness merged and flowed inside her body, building up to an intensity that she longed to release. Suddenly his fingers pushed inside her and she cried out, her body flexing over his fingers that stayed there, playing, rolling around her wetness before releasing her and massaging her, making her legs suddenly weak.

He held her in his arms while he slid on a condom. Then he pressed his body against hers, lifted her and slid straight into her as she wrapped her legs tight around him. He was so strong; it was as if she were nothing in his arms. She wrapped her arms around his neck and pressed her mouth to his skin, tasting the residue of the salt and sweat that slowly drained away, leaving only the essence of him.

He filled her inside and outside: it was as if she was being consumed by him and, yet, at the same time she felt as if she were consuming him—they were one. And again, came as one together.

As the light slowly filled the room, Lucy lay quietly in Razeen's arms, listening to the soothing murmur of the calm ocean below the Lodge and the wild call of some exotic bird flying overhead. She'd never felt so sated, so complete, so... at home.

"You have just two more weeks here before your return?"

His words hit her like a body blow. Was he seeking reassurance that she wouldn't become a clingy lover? He wanted the end defined after the night they'd shared together?

"Yes, just two more weeks. Then I must go." She risked a quick look at him. He appeared more relaxed, as if a decision had been made. She sighed and gazed out at the sea. "I love the sea."

"Perhaps you're a mermaid, a siren of the seas. That would explain..."

Uncharacteristically, he didn't complete his sentence. "Explain what?"

Slowly the shadows drifted away, absorbed by the light, until the familiarity of the dark dissolved into the strange reality of the day. She shifted away slightly. He stopped stroking her arm and moved so he could see her face. "What is it about the sea that fascinates you?"

"It takes you away." She hesitated. "I was brought up by the coast. I used to look out over the sea wall at the darkness of the sea and wish I were on it. So I could keep on moving."

"You were unhappy then, at home?"

She nodded, not trusting herself to speak.

"You can't go on moving forever. There's nothing that would make you stay."

Was it a question or a statement? She didn't know. She shook her head in his arms.

He paused a moment before slipping his arm from under her. He kissed her lightly and rose. "Good. It fits with my plans. I will be busy in two weeks' time."

"Two weeks it is then."

Two weeks, she repeated in her mind, wondering at the confusion of feelings the two words engendered. She didn't *do* commitment, she reminded herself. She couldn't—not after what happened. But, for the first time since she was fifteen she felt vulnerable and it wasn't a good feeling: like a heavy boot, digging into her gut, reminding her of the pain that lay just below the surface. It was just as well he was a commitment-phobe as she had no intention of releasing the pain of her youth.

"It'll be daylight soon. We must leave soon. I've cancelled most of my appointments, but I've a few meetings at the palace I must attend."

"Sure." She watched him move around the room, his broad, well-muscled body almost a taupe-grey in the dim light. He had an ease of movement she'd noticed in his people, which must have been inherited from his people: a sure-footedness, a grace, despite his height and powerful build.

But she also sensed something else. He'd moved away from her slightly. She swung her legs off the bed and pushed her fingers through her unruly hair. She couldn't regret their night together. It had been the most magical of her life. He'd made her no promises and she'd told him in no uncertain terms she would be leaving in two weeks. It had been magic but she knew magic couldn't continue, didn't she? It wouldn't be magic if it did.

Lucy *had* to tell Razeen the real reason she was here. Now she knew him better, now she trusted him and knew he spoke the truth when he said he invited no one here. But for some reason she hesitated. How would he respond to her suspicions?

"We'd better move, Lucy. I'm late. We'll breakfast at the palace."

"Sure. I'm ready when you are." Lucy's smile was met with a light kiss and a narrowed gaze. "I travel light."

He slipped his hands around her body and pulled her to him. "We'll have to stop at the pontoon to collect your bikini on the way." All thoughts of the confession that hovered on her tongue, fled at the memory of last night. She wasn't inhibited but the thought of their love-making on the beach brought a blush to her cheeks. She grinned and looked down.

His unshaved cheek brushed roughly against hers, as his lips found hers. "Just the thought of you slipping naked through the water makes me want to postpone my meetings." He kissed her long and hard. "You're a bad influence on me, making me forget who I am, what I have to do."

"Works two ways. I have very important things to do too, you know."

"Such as?"

Lucy drew in a deep breath. She had to tell him. "Razeen, I—"

The phone rang but Razeen didn't move. "Go on."

"I came here for a purpose."

"Yes, of course you did. Sitra isn't somewhere one comes to by accident. You wanted to experience a new culture, do a bit of sight seeing. Isn't that what you said?"

The phone continued to ring, unrelenting and urgent.

"That wasn't the reason. I was, I *am*, looking for someone."

He frowned. "I didn't think you knew anyone here?" His frown deepened. "A friend, lover? Who?"

The continuous shrill ringing of the phone, together with a change to the tone of his voice—suspicion, jealousy—conspired to constrict her throat. Tension coiled inside her. "None of the above."

"Good." His frown faded and he shrugged and walked off to answer the phone.

"Razeen, I must—"

He held up his hand. "One moment, Lucy."

He spoke rapidly in Arabic before looking up at her. "I won't be long."

She sighed, frustrated that her attempt at telling Razeen about Maia had been lost, and wandered off.

The previous evening and night had been so intimate with Razeen—physically and emotionally—she felt she knew him. But she didn't know him. There was a hint of something in his voice, jealousy or irritation, when she'd said she'd another reason for coming to Sitra that disturbed her. How would he respond to her distrust of him, her suspicions? But she had to tell him because she needed his help. Now that he wasn't a suspect, she needed to find out what exactly had happened to Maia after the photo had been taken.

She wandered over to the bookshelves and trailed her hands

bumpily along the rows of books. Her sister would have loved it here. She'd been the bookworm in the family. This was just the sort of place she'd make a beeline for.

She heard Razeen's deep voice in the background, the language flowing and rolling between his lips like a river tumbling easily over smooth rocks. It was a very peaceful language, Lucy decided. She smiled to herself at the fanciful thought and continued to walk alongside the bookshelves until she came to a window seat piled with books. She sat and crossed her legs on the seat. She was practically hidden here behind a swag of curtain and the books. She leaned back on the cushions and scanned the horizon. It was slightly rougher, but the skies were as blue as ever. She wondered if Razeen had been mistaken about a storm coming. Only the increased swell of the sea suggested anything was brewing. The pontoon was bobbing with more vigor this morning. She grinned at the thought of her bikini lying there and flushed at the thought of their lovemaking.

To distract herself she picked up one of the books that lay on top of a small pile and frowned. It was one she remembered from her childhood—her mother had used to read it to her. And then after her mother had died, her sister had read it to her, even when they were much older. The memory of those times, of the tight bond between the two sisters and of their shared sorrow filled her, and she pulled out the book and flicked it open. It was an even older version of the book than they'd had at home. She let it fall open in her hands and she stared, stunned at what she was looking at.

A bookmark. But not just any bookmark. It was made of a long strip of well-worn leather finished at each end with a small token. Lucy smoothed her fingers over the small ceramic image of the kiwi bird, whose color was almost rubbed off and pulled the other end free of the book, her heart pounding so loudly that Razeen's sonorous voice and the dull roar of the surf on the beach were drowned out. At the other end of the bookmark was a dolphin. The end of its tail had been snapped off.

She pressed it between her fingers, disbelieving for several long moments. She rubbed her thumb over the worn end of the dolphin's tail. She remembered the day Maia had broken it. Lucy had been so cross because she'd saved the money and bought it for Maia. The dolphin represented Lucy and the kiwi was just like Maia, because she came alive at night. She turned it back and forth in her hand. There were no two ways about it. It was Maia's bookmark.

Maia had been here. Maia had been drawn to the books, like Lucy knew she would have been. And Maia had picked up the book, drawn by the same memories as herself. Maia had stood where she was standing and…then what? Had she left in a hurry? Left with whom? Razeen?

A wave of nausea filled her. Razeen had lied. He'd damn well lied and she'd fallen for it. Just as Maia had no doubt fallen for his charm. Her head pounded and she dropped her head in her hands, holding it tight, willing herself to calm, to edge out the panic and think straight. A door slammed closed behind her and Lucy jumped up, her heart beating a rapid tattoo as adrenalin surged through her body.

"Lucy?"

By the time he checked the window seat, Lucy's panic had subsided and the book was back on the pile, but with a page no longer marked. Lucy's hand patted her pocket just to make sure and she fingered the outline of the kiwi.

Don't worry, night bird, I'm coming for you.

"You ready?"

She looked up at him, into the face of the stranger he truly was. But she nodded, determined, now more than ever to find her sister. He'd soon find out just how ready.

CHAPTER SEVEN

The sea heaved under the boat with a menace that reflected the turmoil of suspicion and guilt that filled her. While Razeen guided the boat across the crests of the quickened waves, Lucy searched the shoreline—not visible in last night's darkness—wondering where Maia might be.

They stopped only to maneuver alongside the pontoon to collect her bikini which he tossed into the boat with a brief smile that quickly became a frown. He obviously sensed her withdrawal; she'd never been good at hiding her feelings. She turned away, tormented by the confusion that raged within her. On the one hand she couldn't help watching his muscles bulk out as he pulled hard on the rudder, her fingers flexing as she contained an urge to reach out and touch him. And yet on the other, she was sickened by her physical responses, in the knowledge that she'd betrayed her sister.

She looked toward the palace, gleaming under the harsh sunlight. She'd grown sloppy, grown weak under the spell of this man, this stranger. But she'd be on the alert for Maia now. She'd keep on looking by herself, just for a few days and then, if she'd made no progress, she'd have to ask Razeen. But not now. Only when she knew Alex, and an escape, was available to her. She didn't know Razeen: she thought she did, but she didn't. Who knew what he was capable of?

After he'd tied up the boat in the shed

he reached for her hand and she
gazed down at his rich brown skin,
so beautiful, so seductive, but she
couldn't allow herself to do what she so
wanted to do, to curl her fingers around
his hands and feel his grip tighten
around hers.

"What's wrong Lucy?" His brow
lowered, the frown line deepening.

She opened her mouth to speak
but for once her mind was too full of
conflicting thoughts to give voice to
a single one. She shook her head and
turned away.

"Regret getting carried away last
night? Or is it something to do with the
person you're looking for. I was waiting
for you to mention it again. Obviously
you regretted having done so. So many
regrets…" His voice had become hard.

She nodded once. He turned away,
but not before she caught sight
of an expression that held both
disappointment and anger.

"I would never have taken you away if I thought you harbored any doubts."

"I didn't then. You know that. It's just…hard to explain."

"Try."

His cell phone beeped. He swore. "We have to get back. Do you wish to leave Sitra?"

She shook her head vehemently, appalled at the thought that she could leave Sitra before she'd found Maia. "No, not at all."

"Do you wish to see me again?"

She bit her lip, to stop it from trembling. "Yes." She had to. He was still her only lead.

"You sure?"

"Yes. Look, I'm sorry, I'm just not feeling myself this morning."

He stepped away, his face remaining impassive as if he didn't believe her. "I have a few urgent meetings this morning I must attend but I'll see you later. Is there anything you need while

I'm working?" The remote politeness of his enquiry made Lucy wince. But there were more important things she needed than his intimacy.

"Internet access. Can you arrange it for me?"

"Come to my office and see my assistant. He'll give you access to a computer."

They strode quickly up the steps and through the luxuriant gardens dripping with soft morning dew. The gardeners were out in force, trimming and watering, aware the King and his girlfriend were passing by, but obviously too discreet to stare. At the gardens where they were to go their separate ways, he turned to her.

"Talk to me later. Something has happened I don't understand. And I want to, Lucy. Whatever direction your mind is taking you, know this. Last night was special to me. If our time together is short, that's not of my doing. I want you." He pursed his lips together as if wanting to speak further but instead, turned away and left abruptly, without a backward glance.

Once inside her suite of rooms, she leaned back against the door, suddenly exhausted, closed her eyes and groped for the bookmark that was hidden in her pocket, her fingers worrying the soft edges of the kiwi.

Maia...where are you?

* * *

Lucy's fingers hovered over the keyboard as she glanced furtively around the office. Two assistants were working on papers in a corner while a couple of senior advisers were having a meeting in an outer office. There was a hum of printers, keyboard clattering and the distant sound of a phone on loudspeaker. No one was paying her any attention, presumably used to strangers needing their internet fix.

She logged into her Facebook account and scanned its contents for anything from Maia. There she was. She clicked on it and read. She slammed the heel of her hand onto the desk in frustration and quickly scanned the office to see if anyone had noticed. Everyone was still absorbed in his or her own business. She continued to read.

More myths Maia believed would satisfy her. She wrote of parties, of people she was seeing. She wrote of rain; she wrote of Paris. None of it was true. Maia hadn't been seen in Paris for months. Lucy had been there before she'd joined the boat with Alex. She realized if her own investigations failed she'd have to take the next step and try again to get the police involved. She'd spoken to them in Paris but they'd pointed to her Facebook pages as proof that Maia was okay. They'd also pointed out that Maia rarely stayed in one country for more than a few weeks at a time. She could be anywhere.

She shook her head at the lies posted on Maia's Facebook wall. She sent another reply. "Maia, where the hell are you, really?"

She raked her fingers through her hair with frustration as she stared at the laptop. They'd both sworn to each other that they'd live life to the full. Maia had been dead set against a mundane life of husband and children. It hadn't worked for their mother, she'd argued, so why risk it? And, Lucy? Lucy had other reasons not to want to tie herself into a relationship: reasons that she never held up to the light to scrutinize, reasons best left forgotten—that way they couldn't hurt her.

So, for the last eight years they'd kept to that pact. But now? Lucy didn't know what the hell Maia was playing at. The tweets and Facebook messages were designed to allay her fears but, instead, only increased them.

"Damn." She rubbed away a tear of frustration.

"Bad news?"

She nearly jumped out of her skin. Razeen stood directly behind her; somehow the other people in the office had vanished leaving only the two of them.

"No, I was just—"

"Let me see, perhaps I can help? Facebook? A personal matter then?" He began to turn away but caught sight of Maia's photo. "You know this woman?"

Lucy closed her eyes tight. She couldn't put it off any longer. Whatever Razeen was about to do, she'd cope. She needed to know. She opened her eyes and twisted round to meet his puzzled gaze. "This *woman* is my sister."

His face froze under the impact of her words before their full significance filtered through the shock and came to rest in his eyes that deepened in hurt and then went cold. "I knew her in Paris." He stepped back.

She turned to the computer once more and flicked up the photo of him and Maia. "I know."

His expression was so cool it hurt. "From that photograph 'you know', or from Maia?"

"From the photograph." She fiddled with the computer mouse uncertainly, not wanting to continue but knowing she had to. "You were obviously having fun with her."

"Like you think I had 'fun' with you?"

She bit her lip. "I don't know what to think."

"You do, don't you? You believe I had an affair with Maia, and for some reason I cannot begin to fathom, you've come to Sitra, you've come to see me, because of it. Isn't that the truth?"

His voice was as cold and

authoritative as any autocratic ruler about to sit in judgment on a subject, about to condemn a subject.

"Yes."

He sat down and fixed a cold gaze on her. "You cannot assume you know the truth, Lucy, by the existence of a photograph." His voice was deathly quiet, "Ask me about her and I will tell you."

Silence weighed heavily. It was broken only by the whirring of an overhead fan and the distant sound of city traffic. A bead of sweat trickled down her back. The words formed but her throat was dry and scratchy and they didn't emerge. She swallowed and cleared her throat. "Where is she?"

He smiled but it was like no smile she'd seen before. "As direct as usual. Unfortunately I can't answer that to your satisfaction. I don't know where she is."

"Why not?" She jumped up, angry

now, no longer able to sit and stare at this stranger who held the key to so much information she needed.

"As I said, I knew her in Paris. I invited a group of my friends to come to Sitra and she joined us. And, as far as I know, she returned to Paris shortly afterwards."

"She came here with your friends. You must know if she left or not."

"She came here with me, along with six others. I was busy, I left them to explore. To my knowledge they all left the country by private boat a week later." He stood up from the chair and strode to the window, his fingers rubbing his head in confusion. "Are you trying to tell me she never made it home? What about those updates posted on Facebook?" He strode over to the computer again. "That one was posted only days ago."

"It's a lie. All the posts for the last few months have been lies. I've been to Paris. I've checked with the people, been to the places. No one has seen her. The last genuine post is the photo of you and her. Just the two of you, Razeen. It was over four months ago. I've not heard from her since."

"Then what are the posts you've been looking at? Who are they from, if not her?"

"I don't know. The police won't do a thing. They say the posts are proof she's alive and well. They say not replying to messages isn't an indication anything's wrong." She continued to pace. "They say it's an indication she doesn't want to contact me. But..." She took a deep breath in a vain effort to stop herself from breaking down in front of the man who was the prime suspect. He was the only person who could simultaneously give her comfort and yet of whom she was afraid. "But, they're wrong."

"Are you sure about that?"

She bit her lip. "Of course." She had to be. The thought of Maia not wanting to contact her was too awful to contemplate. She stopped pacing and turned to him. "Razeen, help me, please. I'm scared. I think something terrible might have happened to my sister. Please, tell me where she is…" Her voice faded to a whisper.

He gazed down at her with a complex expression that still held reserve but which now also held sympathy. "I don't know where she is now. As I said, I was in Paris with a group of friends. She joined us and we all came to Sitra. That's the last I saw of her, at the palace. I had one of my assistants arrange travel for them wherever they wished to go. They returned by private boat after a week. I did not check up to see who returned, who stayed. I am not a border official. I had work to do. *That*, is the truth."

"Tell me, I have to know. Did you…did

she…"

"Were we lovers?" His dark eyes searched her face as if he were asking something more than a confirmation of her question. She nodded uncertainly. His lips compressed into a heavy line. "No. She was beautiful and fun but I had other things on my mind at the time. I can't speak for others in the party."

"You know something; you must know something. Did she seem close to anyone else?"

He shrugged. "Possibly. She's very lovely and a number of my friends were interested."

"Razeen." She reached into her pocket and withdrew the bookmark. "I found something at the Lodge this morning." She held it up.

"A cheap souvenir?" He looped it around his finger and brought it closer to him.

"That's right. A cheap souvenir from

my hometown. A cheap souvenir that belonged to Maia, that I paid for her with money saved from my job. It was tacky, it was cheap and it meant the world to Maia. What the hell was it doing in your Lodge?"

He let it drop from his hands. "In truth, Lucy, I don't know. But I'll find out."

Lucy watched as Razeen called to his advisers and they came running. She watched as he sent them out to their computers and phones with specific requests, barked out in a language Lucy couldn't understand and that had lost its softness. She watched as he turned back to face her, his expression stern.

"Come." When she didn't move he took her hand. "Come!" He said more loudly.

Lucy still wasn't sure if she trusted Razeen. Her body screamed she could; her mind turned one way and then another as it examined and re-examined his words, his attitude, his meaning, expressed and unexpressed. But it was as if the past half hour had built a wall between them. All she knew was that he was angry.

"I want to know—"

"Leave it to my staff. They'll find out all there is to know." He took her hand and pulled her toward the door.

"But—"

"We need to talk, and not here."

She looked around helplessly as people busily keyed information into computers and spoke on phones. Her shoulders slumped. There was nothing she could do now. Rightly or wrongly, she'd handed over control to Razeen.

Still with her hand in his she followed him out of the office. They walked through lengthy corridors until they came to the gardens outside her suite of rooms. She sat down and he paced up and down in front of her.

"You lied to me, Lucy. Everything was a pretense, wasn't it? All of it. Because you thought me capable of seducing your sister, and worse."

She shook her head. "It wasn't like that, I—"

"Don't give me that," he shouted angrily. "You slept with me, you made love to me, all the while knowing you didn't trust me an inch." He shook his head. "You're incredible."

"It wasn't like that. I believed you when you said no one had stayed with you at the Lodge before me. I believed that. It was only then that I allowed myself to relax with you, to allow my feelings, my body, to take over."

He stood over her. "I don't believe you. How can I believe anything you say again? If you came all this way to check me out, why would a few words from me alleviate your fears? You're lying again."

She shook her head, unable to frame

the words that would convince him.

"Trust, Lucy, has been in short supply in my life. Therefore I value it. It's basic economics: supply and demand."

Lucy rose slowly, feeling anger mount with every unjust word. "You can't demand trust—it's earned."

"No, you're wrong. It goes deeper than that. It reflects your own insecurities, just as it reflected my father's." His mouth twisted with uncharacteristic uncertainty, as if he'd said more than he intended to. "I don't take responsibility for other people's distrust any longer." His cold gaze held hers. "I judge them by it. I judge *you* by it."

She swallowed, suddenly afraid, not for herself physically but for what she might have just lost. He began to walk away. "Razeen," she reached out for him. "What the hell was I meant to think? You were the only link to Maia."

"And you made love to me, Lucy,

knowing you distrusted me." He shook his head. "What kind of woman are you?"

"Please." She reached out again, found his arm and gripped it tight, as if the connection was everything.

He stood still. "What? What is it you want?"

"I want," she swallowed hard. There were so many things she wanted, she *needed*, from Razeen. But none she could speak of because she had to put herself second. While Razeen might not know what happened to Maia, he was the only one who could help her find her. Because she knew, just knew, that Maia was in Sitra somewhere. "I want, I *need*, your help. I *have* to find Maia."

He looked down at her hand on his arm. "And that's all you want, is it?" He sighed at her brief nod. "I'll help you find her. Of course I will. I don't want people disappearing without trace in my country." He closed his eyes momentarily. "Rest assured, Lucy. I will help you. I have people working on it now. Go now. Eat. Rest. If she's anywhere in Sitra I will find her easily enough. And if she's in France, or wherever," he shrugged, "well, that may take a little longer but I'll get as much information for you as I can."

"Thank you."

His eyes were hard now, so different to how they'd been earlier.

"Now," he pulled his arm away, "do whatever you wish but I must go."

He turned and left her without a backward glance. Lucy felt grief fill the pit of her stomach like cold stone: grief for her lost sister and grief for the loss of the spark that had filled Razeen's eyes when he'd looked at her. Now, all she saw was disappointment and anger.

Lucy went inside her suite and lay on the bed. Her fingers sought the bookmark and she rubbed its smooth surface between her fingers, desperate for comfort.

I'm coming, Maia, I'm coming.

After an afternoon of pacing her rooms, Lucy was sitting on the bed, her head in her hands, there was a knock at the door. She leaped up to answer it and found a weary Razeen standing there, hands thrust in pockets, eyes guarded.

"Prepare yourself for a journey. I think I may have found her."

"Where? Is she all right? Tell me!"

"I don't know the details. Just a lead. Get your things."

Lucy had already prepared her bag and within minutes she was following Razeen down to the garages. They were soon roaring across the desert in a four-wheel drive, followed by another vehicle containing his bodyguards.

Lucy glanced repeatedly at Razeen, willing him to speak. But his lips were clamped together in an expression of grim determination. She followed his gaze out to the flat desert—more a stony plain than the sand dunes she'd imagined—and the distant mountains that were a startling orange in the afternoon sun. There was nothing but emptiness for miles upon miles. Wherever their destination, she could see it would be a long journey. She just prayed that Maia was all right, that Razeen was silent because of his anger with her, not because anything bad had happened to Maia.

The four-wheel drive revved and roared over the bumpy ground and she clung to the door handle. The air conditioning was on low and it was warm and dry in the vehicle. She drank from her water bottle but it did nothing to ease her discomfort. She couldn't bear the tension any longer.

"Razeen, you may be disappointed in me, you may hate me, but you have to tell me. What do you know?" Her voice was cracked with emotion.

He didn't answer immediately, merely focused on the dirt road ahead.

She took a deep breath. "Please. Give me something. Tell me she'd not dead."

He glanced at her, but the expression in his eyes wasn't reassuring. "She's not dead."

Lucy fell back against the seat with relief. "Thank God."

"I have accounted for all of my party except for one of the domestic staff at the Lodge with whom Maia was friendly. The man is a Bedouin from the place we are going to. I'm hoping he may be able to tell us where she is."

Panic filled her. "Why? Does he have a criminal record? What kind of man is he?"

"I would hardly employ someone at the Lodge if he had a criminal record." Razeen shrugged. "By all accounts he is hard worker, an intelligent man, who returned to his home around the same time my party of friends left."

"And you're sure they left without her?"

"Positive. I checked with them all. My friends all confirm she arrived here with them, that she stayed at the Lodge with them, but she didn't leave with them."

"You contacted them! Why didn't you tell me? What did they say?"

"It appears she took a liking to the waiter, Mohammed, who I haven't been able to contact."

Lucy let out a breath she didn't know she'd been holding. "Waiter? Oh no, that's not possible. She likes the high life."

"I doubt very much that Mohammed would have been able to take her away unless she'd been willing. There's no indication from my friends that she wasn't willing."

She groaned. "She couldn't have been willing. Why the hell would she leave the life she'd been living—that

197

held everything she'd always wanted—
and disappear into the desert with
some, some gypsy servant, waiter,
whatever?"

"They are not gypsies," he said
patiently. "They are an ancient people
with honorable ways. Just because you
do not know of them, do not suppose
they are without value."

"I'm sorry," she rubbed her eyes. "I'm
just so scared. How much further?"

"We are going to the mountains
directly ahead, at the end of this road."

"I can't see how you can make out a
road here. It all looks the same."

"Just as well you're not driving then."

He shifted his glance—as stony and
arid as the landscape surrounding
them—back to the road ahead. Lucy
turned away feeling sick to her
stomach, not only with apprehension
over Maia but with how her intimacy
with Razeen had turned into suspicion
and distrust.

Hours past and Lucy watched a group of buzzards circling high overhead. Life was hard in the desert. She couldn't imagine her glamorous sister here. Razeen was wrong. He had to be.

"We'll stop for the night shortly."

"No, please. We must get to Maia tonight. Can't we keep going?"

"It's too far. We started out too late. We'll pitch our tents in the next oasis tonight and leave at first light. Then, tomorrow we'll reach our destination. If she's there, we'll find her."

"But if she's not?"

"Then I'll continue to make enquiries until I know where she is—inside and outside of Sitra."

"Thank you." Razeen might be angry with her, he might be barely civil but she knew his sense of honor wouldn't allow him to give up on her search for Maia. Inside she grieved for what might have been but she was just thankful he was helping her.

"Tell me about her, anything that could help," Razeen continued.

"Maia had—*has*—everything she ever wanted: a great career as a model, wealth, fun. She loved life and loved living it to the full."

"Perhaps having everything she ever wanted wasn't enough."

"You don't know her like I do. You don't know what our life was like."

"Then tell me."

She was silent for a few moments. "It was hard for me but it was harder for Maia. Mum died when Maia was sixteen. Dad came back and wanted us to go and live with him but she wouldn't go. She told him to get out like he'd done when we were young. She wouldn't have anything to do with him. She left school, got a job and paid the bills and looked after me." Lucy swallowed and took a deep breath. She'd told few people about her past but now she had no choice. "It wasn't always easy

200

for her. I had a mind of my own, my own issues, my own problems. But she always cared for me. Did what she could. And then, stuff happened, I left school and we made a pact: to never compromise, to lead a different life to the one our mother led. Maia was wonderful to me, always. She is..."

Lucy couldn't go on. The tears threatened and the last thing she wanted was to breakdown in front of Razeen. She stared out the window until her eyes burned, trying to hide her emotion from him but his hand covered her own fisted hand and squeezed it.

"We *will* find her."

Lucy pulled her free hand to her mouth to try to stifle the sobs that hitched in her throat while leaving her other hand in the warm grip of Razeen. She felt as if she were disintegrating. After being independent for so long, being strong through everything, to have the man beside her give her comfort brought the tears to the surface.

"Don't cry, Lucy. All will be well."

"I never cry," she sobbed, somehow managing to prevent the tears from flowing. "I don't cry. That's weak. I'm not weak."

"Even the strong cry sometimes."

It was as if his words triggered all the fear that had been tied in a knot in the pit of her stomach for so long and when she opened her mouth to speak only a wail, a cry of despair, filled the car.

CHAPTER EIGHT

The oasis was filled with the eerie sound of the rabab being played by one of his men. The man was singing of loss and longing and Razeen felt the man's emotion with every pass of the bow across the single string. Razeen shifted his back against the thick trunk of the date palm and gazed across the darting flames of the fire at Lucy, her plate of food untouched before her.

If she'd been surprised at his reaction to her revelation, then he'd been more surprised. His affair with Lucy was meant to have been a no-ties fling on both sides; a short interlude before his life changed course. Then why had her lack of trust in him thrown him so completely?

He turned away, unable to watch her any longer. He took a long drink of hot tea and wished he'd brought something stronger, something that would have numbed the unwelcome feelings that had surfaced from nowhere and refused to leave. She got to him. She uncovered the hurt of his youth—when his father had shown him how little he believed in him—that he could have sworn he'd forgotten.

He looked across to his men who were grouped around a second fire, alternately singing and drinking. He envied them their apparent simplicity. Then he tilted his head slowly until only the stars were visible between the leaves of the ragged palm fronds. He recited the names of the different star groups out of habit. He'd used to ride out into the desert to escape his father, then stay out all night to make his father worry. He hadn't though. His father hadn't bothered to try to find him. It had been his staff who had gone looking for him. His father hadn't cared.

"What are you looking at?" Lucy's voice was soft on the quiet night air.

"The stars." He didn't look at her but heard her move around the fire toward him.

"You're a romantic at heart."

"You don't know me," he snapped back, the deep-seated bitterness lashing out in an attack he immediately regretted. Then he turned to her and his heart stopped. Her hair tumbled around her shoulders and her eyes were huge in the flickering light of the fire. She looked so vulnerable it made his unromantic heart ache.

"No, I don't. It was just an observation." She pushed her hands through her already untidy hair. "Look, I'm tired, I don't want to argue. I'm going to bed."

He reached out and grabbed her hand and was shocked by the way she jumped. "Wait, I'm sorry. For all of this, I'm sorry."

"It's not your fault Maia disappeared into the desert with a stranger."

"No, but it's my fault I was angry with you for your lack of trust in me."

She shook her head incredulously. "But I *did* trust you; I trusted the man on the beach, that first night; I trusted Razeen."

"What do you mean?"

"I could have turned tail, swam back to the boat. After all I was alone, wearing only a bikini, with a strange man. But… I trusted you. Instinctively I trusted you." She shifted her gaze to the fire whose flames danced in the darkness. "And I was right. You were, you are, wonderful: so caring, so respectful."

He drew in a ragged breath that

contained the subtle scent of her skin and stood up, unable to stop himself. He pushed his fingers through her unruly hair so he could see her face and brought his lips to hers, needing to connect with her, needing to give back to her what she'd just given him. She melted in his arms. And the feeling of her body, so soft and warm, folding against his hard body, ignited a fire deep within him. He deepened the kiss, needing to feel her tongue against his own, her breath mingling with his. He groaned as she slid her hands around his waist and pressed her hips against his. He pulled away sharply, still holding her face in his hands.

"Are you sure you want this? Tell me now if you don't."

She covered his hand with her own. "Razeen, come to me?" Her voice sounded small and tentative, lost in the empty hollowness of the vast desert. Even the men's singing was silent now. He took her hand and they walked swiftly through the warm sand of the oasis to his tent.

Once inside, darkness enveloped them and there was nothing but the delicate scent of Lucy's skin, the feel of her curves under his hands, and the taste of her lips. He laid her gently onto the bed and slowly unbuttoned her top. She gasped as his fingers brushed against her sensitive skin and she arched back when he pushed her bra aside and claimed her breast with his mouth. He'd made love so many times in his life and yet it had never felt like this.

The silence and darkness of the desert, that weighed heavily all around them, combined with the emotional turmoil of the past twelve hours to create an intensity of experience that heightened every sense. Everything appeared so simple now, in this timeless place where only he and Lucy existed.

Within seconds they'd both shed their clothes and he swept his hands up her naked body as she angled herself for him. He knelt back and watched her as he rolled on the condom. Then, gently he slid inside her, dipped down to her lips and kissed her. Their mouths didn't leave one another's as he moved, slowly at first, inside her. He took his lead from her: the movement of her hands over his body, the breath that quickened in his mouth, and the heat of her skin against his. Never had he felt so in tune with another person.

With all external thoughts and senses closed down—no sight in the darkness, nothing but the stillness of the desert outside the tent—he knew Lucy only through his body that moved instinctively in and against hers. Together they edged toward that bliss that lay like a flower, furled and waiting, only released into bloom by the communion of their bodies.

Lucy awoke with a start. She couldn't think where she was for a moment. Slowly she searched the grey, pre-dawn light that crept in around the flaps of the tent. Then she remembered. She sat bolt upright, her heart thumping; the cold desert air sweeping over her like an icy cloak. Today, she'd see Maia.

The muttered prayers of the men and the smell of smoke from the re-kindled fire drifted into the tent. She lay back onto the soft pillow and turned to where Razeen had lain beside her. There was nothing but an indentation on the pillow. She reached out and touched it, curving the back of her hand where his head had lain. It was still warm. She closed her eyes and remembered the long night of murmured talking, of quiet touching and lovemaking. Somehow, despite her habitual insomnia, she'd fallen asleep in his arms. She hadn't expected to. But she'd felt so safe, so content. Guilt swept through her. What was she doing sleeping in someone's arms when her sister could be out there in the cold, needing her?

She leaped up and pulled on her clothes quickly, overlaying them with the abaya, as much for warmth as modesty, and looked outside. Razeen was with the handful of men he'd brought with him. They'd finished their prayers and were busy preparing food. But Lucy didn't move toward them. She wanted to be on her own.

The sky was completely clear of cloud, and stars still littered its inky heights but the faintest blush of red lit the eastern horizon. Even while her stomach was tied in knots with anxiety about her sister, Lucy couldn't help be aware of the massive silence around her. The early light shimmered in its inexorable creep toward dawn.

She pulled the robes more tightly

around her and stepped away from the tent, out further into the blank wilderness that she'd never known to exist. Even when she'd felt at her most isolated, on a small boat in the middle of the Pacific Ocean, there had always been things to do, people to talk to, the noise and sights and smell of the sea. But here, there was simply nothing. And yet it didn't feel diminishing, it felt curiously enriching. It wasn't an empty peace; it was a rich, replete peace.

Slowly she turned a full circle looking up at the night sky that was suddenly shot with vivid fiery red, the flame extinguishing the light of the stars almost at once. Then she turned back to the camp where, through air that lightened with each passing minute, she saw Razeen silently watching her. She smiled briefly, tentatively, although he wouldn't see her from that distance, just as she couldn't decipher his expression. But she knew what he was feeling because somehow, he'd seeped under her skin, in the same way the light was penetrating the darkness, just as the silence was finding its hold within her.

She turned to look up at the stars once more but they'd vanished under the fiery glow of the still hidden sun. She turned to Razeen but he was also gone. She didn't know what was happening with him. But today wasn't a day to find out. Today was all about Maia.

After a quick breakfast, they were on their way again, bumping across the uneven desert, this time following the other vehicle. The only feature to break the empty expanse was the mountain range toward which they were headed.

"I've never been anywhere so remote."

"If you think this is remote, you should visit Qawaran, Zahir's kingdom.

It's landlocked but with an ancient heritage."

"This is remote enough, believe me. Do you really think Maia is near here?"

"The city of caves is high up in the mountain ahead. The Bedouin there are cave dwellers."

Lucy tried to imagine where she was going but failed. She rolled her head around the head rest and surveyed the miles and miles of unvarying landscape. "She can't be there. It's just not like her. But if it's not her, we've come to a dead end again."

"Maybe; maybe not. We won't know until we get there. If she's not there, then perhaps someone will be able to tell us where to go next."

"Perhaps." With the coming of the daylight Lucy's confidence had waned. Now it had almost totally disappeared. This wasn't the kind of place she thought she'd ever find Maia: Maia, who loved fine clothes, sparkling company, a fun time. Despair engulfed her. "No, not 'maybe'. She's *not* here. I've taken you from your work on a wild goose chase. I've wasted your time. You may as well turn around."

"Don't be hasty, Lucy. Let's follow this lead and see where it takes us."

She groaned. "What were your friends thinking of, leaving her there?"

"She's a grown woman. She's, what, mid to late 20s? From all accounts she doesn't drink alcohol—"

"Never has—"

"And doesn't take drugs. She was in full command of her faculties. She made a decision to go somewhere of her own accord. My friends respected that and so must you."

"Then tell me why the hell didn't she let me know?"

He shook his head. "That's what I don't understand. Is there any reason you can think of why she wouldn't?"

She huffed. "Apart from the fact

I wouldn't have approved of her wandering off into the desert alone—"

"I don't think she was alone—"

"I can't think why she wouldn't have told me."

"So she knew you'd disapprove?"

Lucy was silent for a moment as she remembered all the times that she'd expressed her disapproval of Maia's lifestyle.

"And that disapproval would have hurt her, irritated her, or angered her?" Razeen continued.

Silence filled only with the roar of the four-wheel drive hung in the air for long moments. "Hurt her," she whispered.

She felt his eyes upon her, just as Maia's would have been: condemning her for her judgment of her sister.

"I think you have your answer as to why she sent you messages to reassure you she was safe, but which covered her real tracks."

"You don't understand. My sister is...

she's a sucker for beautiful things. I worry about her."

"She looked after you, didn't she? For how long?"

"From when she was fourteen really until we left New Zealand with some money she'd demanded from my father." She bit her lip. "Five years."

"And so perhaps she wants to break out a little now. Follow her own interests, find out what she wants."

"She's not *your* sister. I *know* her."

"People change, Lucy. Sometimes people are not who we think they are."

"Not Maia. Not Maia," she repeated softly.

Maia couldn't change. She'd been her one unvarying point of reference her whole life. Her lifeline. They may have chosen to go separate ways but she was always there for her—at the end of a computer, at the end of a telephone. She *needed* her to be there. Lucy would be lost without her. Even now she felt that loss, stirring in the pit of her stomach, sickening her with fear. All her hopes were pinned on what she'd find in the city of caves.

She fixed her gaze on the mountains ahead that grew larger with each mile they drove. The changes were subtle at first but slowly they took form—revealing their texture, dips and shadows—as if they were ancient living creatures, awakening.

Eventually they arrived and began to wend their way up the side of a dry wadi, a steep track with a long vertical drop to a dry riverbed. For an hour they climbed until they reached a plateau, encircled by higher mountains still. They slowed and Lucy looked around, puzzled.

"Are we here? Is this it?"

"That's why it was a successful stronghold: invisible and defensible. You see over there where the rocks seem lighter, that's the entrance."

They drove toward the cliff and still Lucy couldn't see the entrance. It wasn't until they were immediately upon it that she saw it overlapped and, in what appeared to be a continuous cliff face, there was an opening. They drove around the projecting cliff and turned into a narrow valley. It ran only for a short while before suddenly opening out into a huge amphitheater in the middle of which was a lush oasis and a collection of stone buildings. The vehicles pulled up in a cloud of dust. Lucy surveyed the empty valley and her heart sank.

"There's no one here."

"They're here all right. Come on, let's go and find your sister."

Lucy closed her eyes at his words as she tried to contain the feelings of hope and fear that raged inside. Then she jumped out. The oasis was lush and beautiful; the buildings, ancient and frustratingly empty. She turned back to the cliff face and narrowed her eyes. Set in the stunning earthen orange of the near vertical cliffs, were irregularly dotted black holes.

She followed Razeen to the cliffs, flanked by his men who automatically fell into defense formation around them both. At first the place appeared empty—the only sounds being the overhead cry of a hawk disturbed from its hunt and the clatter of the palm leaves as they swayed in the light breeze—but as they grew closer she saw the dark holes were cave entrances. But still no sign of people until Lucy saw the shimmer of light on the stone face coalesce into the form of a man. Then a group of men stepped forward, seemingly out of a sheer wall. Then the details revealed themselves. Carved out of the rock face in front of the openings were small terraces, complete with plants, tables and chairs. Beyond the sheer rock face lay a city.

Within moments greetings were called, and the men—dressed traditionally in billowing white dishdasha robes and checkered keffiyehs, complete with ceremonial knives in honor of their visitors—mingled with Razeen's men. With loud shouts of greeting, the strangers ushered them to the caves.

Lucy impatiently searched for signs of Maia. But there were none.

"Where are the women?" Lucy whispered to Razeen as he listened to the sheikh's rapid flow of talk.

Razeen barked out a few words to the local sheikh, and a woman swathed in a black abaya and niqab emerged from one of the caves. Perhaps this woman would know where Maia was. God, she hoped so. She had so many questions.

Then the woman stopped in front of her, her kohl-encircled eyes searching Lucy's.

"Don't you recognize me, Luce?"

Shock slammed into her as the woman stepped up to Lucy and brought her arms around her. Stunned, Lucy couldn't move, couldn't speak just moved her cheek against the woman's cheek and whispered, "Maia?" She pulled back, gripping the other woman on both arms. "Is it really you?"

"It's me, Lucy." She pulled off her niqab to reveal a perfect oval face, a smile bursting with happiness and green eyes as direct and intelligent as ever.

Tears suddenly flowed down Lucy's face. For too long she'd been trying to keep them in; for too long she'd suppressed the fear that something dreadful had happened to Maia; for too long a selfish fear had gripped her that she was, truly, alone.

"Hush," Maia soothed as she pulled Lucy once more into her arms. It was as if Lucy was twelve years old again, bullied by the other girls at school for her lack of cool clothes, her oddness, her skinniness, with only Maia's words of wisdom and arms to run to. "Hush, Lucy." Maia pulled away and smoothed Lucy's hair back and smiled comfortingly. "You've grown your hair since I last saw you."

Suddenly Lucy was furious and gripped her too tightly. "Grown my hair! Is that all you can say? Maia, what the hell are you doing here? Are you all right? Have you been hurt?"

"I'm fine. I'm here with Mohammed. I met him on the coast. He was working at a village by a lodge where I was staying with friends."

"You're here because of a man?" Lucy couldn't believe what she was hearing. Razeen had said as much but she hadn't believed him. "Maia! How could you be so selfish? I've been sick with worry."

"I'm sorry, I didn't know what to do for the best. I knew you wouldn't approve but I had to follow my heart. I arranged with a bureau to post regular blog entries for you, to reassure you."

"And they might have done if you'd replied to your posts, if you'd been where you'd said you were. I went and checked. God, Maia, I thought you'd been abducted or something. I thought—"

"Lucy thought I'd abducted you," Razeen interrupted. "But you're well, Maia?"

"Of course." Maia smiled at Razeen. "I last saw you at the airport when you kindly arranged for one of your staff to show us around. You probably weren't even informed we went to the Lodge. But it was there I met Mohammed." She paused looking from one to the other. "Thank you, Razeen—Your Majesty— for bringing Lucy to me."

Razeen smiled at Lucy. "It's been my pleasure."

Maia's gaze first rested on Razeen,

then Lucy. "How did you meet?"

Razeen didn't move his eyes from Lucy. "She emerged from the water one night, like a water sprite. I think she's not comfortable anywhere other than the sea."

Maia laughed. "She was always that way. Even in winter, she'd swim in the sea."

Lucy raised an eyebrow. "If you two have quite finished talking about me, perhaps we could get to the real issue of how long you intend to stay in this place."

Maia smiled thoughtfully. "That, Luce, is complicated. Come and eat with us. The women are busy preparing food."

"But—"

"Luce, the village will be expecting it."

Razeen nodded in agreement and returned to the sheikh of the local tribe who was waiting for him. Maia fixed her scarf back over her face, linked arms with Lucy and they walked up steps to a wide, deep terrace that was obviously used for entertaining guests. The basic furniture was hewn out of the rock. At its centre was a large round table around which colorful woven cushions were strewn. To one side, stone benches were covered with dishes being brought out from the caves. A watercourse from the oasis had been diverted to water the well-established vines that climbed up and over the top of the terrace, their leaves fluttering in the breeze. The air was fragrant with spices—some of which Lucy recognized from her visit to the market—and freshly baked bread.

Maia brought Lucy to a man, tall, dark and extremely handsome, who stood back watching them.

"Lucy, I'd like you to meet Mohammed."

Lucy eyed him suspiciously but shook his hand. He returned her suspicious look.

"Mohammed." Lucy said shortly.

"Welcome to my home." Mohammed said politely but with a definite chill to his almost perfect English.

"You speak English well."

Again the slight curl of his lips. "As do you. It must be something to do with us both being educated in the West."

Maia laughed uncomfortably. "Lucy, Mohammed has worked and studied in England—King Razeen's grandfather established scholarships for promising Bedouin children—but Mohammed decided to return to his country to help his family and his people."

"Please, come and be seated, my father wishes to begin."

Lucy exchanged a quick look with Maia who was seated demurely next to her. Neither spoke as the formalities were exchanged between the Bedouin sheikh and Razeen. But Lucy felt Maia's hand enclose her fist and squeeze it.

After the formalities were over, the feasting began and the men's talk centered on politics and the economy leaving Lucy and Maia to talk uninterrupted. As soon as they could, they excused themselves and Maia showed Lucy around the caves.

Inside were a series of rooms connected by narrow passageways leading further back into the mountain. It was cool and comfortable and surprisingly luxuriously furnished. Maia took her further back until they were in a huge cavernous space. "This is where the people would come when they were under attack. There were stone doors that slid into position and couldn't be seen from the outside. Obviously they've been removed now for safety reasons—"

"Maia, stop. What the hell are you doing here? Tell me truthfully."

Maia awkwardly brushed her hand across the solid walls. "Mohammed, the

228

way of life, the caves. Lucy, I've never felt so happy, so secure, so loved, in all my life."

The comment cut through Lucy like a knife. Her sister was happy *here*, in the middle of nowhere? "Is it the security, then, that makes you so happy?"

"That's part of it. It comes not just from Mohammed, but also from this place. He makes me feel so different about myself. It's like I have nothing to prove, nothing to struggle for, to fight for. I can just be myself and be treasured because of that."

Despite herself, Lucy couldn't help be moved by the far-away look shining in Maia's eyes. But the stronger the light shone, the deeper her fears grew. "Sounds wonderful."

"It is."

Lucy took a deep breath, fixed a polite smile on her face and looked around, trying to hide her own fear.

"Razeen needs to leave tomorrow

morning early if we're to get back to Sitra by nightfall. Are you coming, Maia?" She knew the answer but she had to ask the question anyway.

Maia shook her head, her eyes full of love and sympathy. She took hold of Lucy's hand. "Mohammed was worried you'd persuade me to leave. That's why he was so defensive. But he has no reason to worry because I can't leave. You must understand, Lucy. I've found a life here I never thought I'd have. I love Mohammed so much."

Lucy opened her mouth to speak the words of sadness and loss that filled her but she swallowed instead and drew Maia to her and held her tight. "I'm happy that you're happy."

Maia drew back and cupped Lucy's tense face. "Oh, Luce! That means *so* much. And, just because I choose to live here doesn't mean I won't travel, that I won't see you. I've earned enough money over the past few years to fund not only what I need to do here, but trips to see you. But not for a while."

There was something in Maia's voice that made her frown. "How long a while?"

Maia slid her hands down to her stomach, her fingers fanning out over it. "At least six months. I'm pregnant."

"Pregnant." The word was barely uttered. It fell from Lucy's lips like a lead weight, stirring as it did an unfathomable pain that Lucy had spent the last eight years trying to suppress. She hadn't known it was still there. "You want children after all we said, after all that happened? Look at the spectacular mess our parents made of it." She swallowed the bile that threatened to rise. She had to say it. "Look what happened to me when—"

Maia pressed her fingers against Lucy's lips. "Don't say it. You don't need to go there."

Lucy gulped down a lungful of hot,

dry air, willing the hurt of her past to recede. "What about all our dreams of escape?"

"I have escaped." Maia said simply. "I don't need anything other than Mohammed. The villagers have welcomed me with open arms; they accept me for who I am. Life is hard physically but I can use the money I have saved to drill a second well, a deeper well. It will save people so much time and effort. I'll be able to afford a bus to run to the capital for hospital visits. I'll make a difference here. And I have a man who makes all the difference in the world to me." Maia shook her head. "You don't get it, do you?"

"No. I'm sorry Maia, I don't. I can see you're happy, but to me it just looks like madness."

Suddenly they were aware of someone else present. Razeen stood by the door. "It's not madness for people to freely choose where they wish to be, what they wish to do."

Lucy sighed. "I guess you're right. But that's how it feels to me." Lucy turned from Razeen to Maia once more. "Are you sure, Maia? Think about everything you're leaving behind."

"I'm leaving nothing behind. Everything I want is here."

Mohammed followed Razeen into the room and stood behind Maia, his hands caressing her arms. Silently they gazed into each other's eyes. Maia sighed and glanced at Lucy. If Lucy hadn't known better she'd have imagined the look was a pitying one.

Lucy smiled stiffly at Maia and Mohammed. "Look after her for me, Mohammed."

He nodded and his face relaxed into a genuine smile for the first time. "Of course."

Lucy hadn't lied. She was happy Maia had found happiness with Mohammed but it didn't take away her own feelings of loss. "I think I'll turn in now. We've an early start in the morning and I'm so tired."

"Sleep well, Lucy."

But, as Lucy walked with Razeen through the dark tunnels, she knew sleep would prove elusive. She might have found Maia—might be relieved she was safe and well—but underlying that was a sense she'd lost, not only Maia, but her own bearings.

CHAPTER NINE

Without Razeen, Lucy's insomnia kicked in again with a vengeance. She slept in a room with other women, as tradition demanded, and spent the night thinking of Maia. Occasionally she dozed only to wake suddenly feeling something or someone was missing. She groaned and closed her eyes as she realized she was missing Razeen's arms, his body pressed against hers.

As the first light of day inched its way into the room, Lucy rose, dressed, and carefully picked her way around the beds and out into the soft light of dawn. She needed to see Razeen. She walked down the rough steps and over to the oasis where the light was brighter. There didn't seem to be anyone around and she silently watched the birds and animals gather at the water's edge.

Razeen saw her as soon as he emerged onto the terrace. She appeared a lonely figure in the grey light and he guessed her feelings.

"Your Majesty, I—"

Razeen held up a hand before turning to his host. "I need a little time. I'll return shortly."

Time. He never had enough of it. It was never his own. But now, he needed to be with Lucy.

She was just turning away from the oasis when he came upon her. He opened his arms and she walked into them and held her face tight against his chest. He curled his arms around her, dropped his cheek against the top of her head and breathed in her subtle perfume. His body responded as it always did when he was near her, but stronger than his physical response was his emotional one. He wanted to soothe the turbulent emotions he sensed within her.

"You're sad, Lucy. Why? You've found your sister. She's well, isn't she? She's happy?"

Lucy pulled away from him. "She's happy all right. But I can't believe my city-loving sister would want to stay here. Do you think she's been brainwashed? Drugged or something?"

He shook his head, unable to prevent a smile. "No. She looks like a woman who very much knows her own mind."

"But, our whole lives, we've dreamed of a time when we wouldn't have to put up with second best, when we could create our own world. And she's given up."

"She's chosen what's best for her. Not given up. Why is that so hard to understand?"

"Because if I accept that, then my life has lost its meaning. I thought the point was to keep on going, keep on moving, experiencing, tasting new things, not settling for anything that wasn't exciting and new."

Razeen suddenly saw, in that beautiful face, the face of a young adolescent girl who'd adored her elder sister and had taken the sister's dreams of escape as a literal plan for life. "Nothing stays the same, Lucy. Not for me, not for Maia and not for you. Your life was what you needed at the time. It will change, as you change."

She shook her head and he felt her body tense as if she'd made some kind of decision. "No. I go on doing what I'm doing. It made me happy then and it'll make me happy in the future. I'm never going to be reliant on anyone for my happiness and I can't believe Maia is."

It was what he needed to hear. But

why did it hurt? He relaxed his grip. "That simply means that you haven't found anything or anyone to make you happy yet. But you will."

He kissed the top of her head feeling regret, for his inability to be with her and for her inability to return his feelings. He closed his eyes against the fragrant smell of her hair—wood smoke, faint orange blossom of shampoo and cool morning air—and tried to imprint it on his memory.

"No, it's not for me. Any of this." She looked around, shaking her head and pulled away from Razeen. "I can smell food. We must eat and then leave if we're to reach the city by nightfall."

"You want to return so soon? I could arrange for a driver to come pick you up in a few days?"

She shook her head, her eyes revealing a poignant blend of pain and defiance. "No, I need to go. For now, I need to go. But I'll be back."

"Then you're right, we must leave very soon. The storm is forecast for later today."

A look of doubt flashed across her face, swiftly replaced by a nod of determination. "Let's get going then. I've had enough of storms for a while."

But, as they walked back to the caves, Razeen cast a worried glance at the western horizon that had already grown blurred.

Over breakfast Lucy watched Maia and Mohammed and saw what she hadn't seen the previous night—how much they felt for each other. When the time came to go, Maia fished Lucy's antique compass from inside her abaya and grinned. "Good to see you still wearing mum's compass."

"I always wear it. It reminds me of when we used to look through the world atlas together. She showed me how to use the compass. She'd always wanted to go overseas, explore different countries."

"And never did. She'd have been so happy to see you traveling. And, look here, you've still got the 'Maia' sticker I stuck above due north. Just look for that and you'll know where I am. And where you are…" She looked at Lucy then and Lucy saw the tears in her eyes. "You'll understand some day. I have to do this. I've chosen this because I love Mohammed."

Lucy kissed her. "Then it's the right decision, isn't it? And a brave one. But you were always strong, always knew what you wanted. And I've always trusted you to make the right decision. So I know you have." Lucy pulled Maia into her arms in an exaggerated bear hug to hide the sense of loss that still gripped her. "I'll come back to see you before the baby's due. I'll be with you then."

They hugged one last time and Lucy

climbed into the vehicle.

Maia turned to Razeen. "Look after my little sister. She's so strong, so capable that sometimes she forgets to allow people to care for her."

"I will."

Lucy didn't look back immediately as they took off out of the valley. When she did, she saw nothing but the dust of their vehicles. Maia and her new family were lost to her.

Lucy gazed out at the wide expanse of desert that stretched, like a sea of pale gold, to the distant horizon, while Razeen and his men drove quickly through the monotonous landscape. This is what she did, she thought, absently. Either drifted on a boat controlled by someone else, or was driven in a car by someone else. And there she was, believing she was free. She was just drifting, propelled along by someone else. Her sister, on the other hand, had taken control and had chosen her future.

She glanced at Razeen. His lips formed a hard line and his expression was tense. No doubt he felt as if she'd sent him on a wild goose chase. From his perspective Maia must have seemed just fine. And no doubt it appeared insulting to him that Lucy couldn't believe Maia could be happy in his country. She chanced another look at him—eyes fixed on the road ahead, mouth stern—and tried to contain the hurt at his withdrawal.

It was stupid to feel such things. He'd done more than she'd asked and she'd made it clear she had no interest in being with him beyond a few weeks. Besides he was the King. Why would he be interested in her? No. They had no future together and she'd done what she set out to do, found her sister and now she had to get on with her own life.

She closed her eyes and let the

revving of the engine over the stones and dips of the track blot out her thoughts. She must have dozed off because when she opened them again, she had to squint and refocus. The sun had disappeared and the air was almost brown, clouds pushing their way out of the dense darkness, as if emerging from the end of a massive bubble blower: blood-red on brown. She'd never seen anything like it.

"What the hell is that?" She sat forward, peering at the expanse before them.

"It's the khamseen." Razeen glanced at her and for the first time she noticed he didn't look merely tense, he looked worried. "We knew one was forecast but it's moving more quickly than we thought."

"Will we get back to the city in time?"

"Let's hope so, or else we'll be lost. We rely on the compasses for navigation." He tapped the one in the car. "The khamseen brings electrical disturbances that makes them useless."

Lucy's hand gripped the compass that hung around her neck. A frisson of fear ran through her body. "Right." She stared at the apparition that appeared like some enormous living being— terrible and majestic—as the clouds continued to spew forth upwards, as if ejected from a giant volcano. "So how far is the city now?"

"An hour away." He glanced at her and mustered a grim smile. "But don't worry, Lucy. We'll get to the city in time."

But she could tell by the way he gripped the steering wheel his words were designed to reassure, not to tell the truth.

"And if we don't?"

He shrugged. "We will have to sit it out. But we *will* get there in time. It's moving fast upon the city. But then, so are we."

"So it's a toss-up as to who gets there first."

He didn't answer as he shifted gears to get the vehicle up a particularly steep incline. From the top of the incline she could see the city—all soft ochre and sand tones—vulnerable in the path of the oncoming storm that massed red and terrible now, obliterating from sight everything behind it as it grew into a massive wall of whirling sand.

"There are scarves in the back, wrap one around your head and mouth."

Lucy didn't question him. She plucked a couple of scarves and wrapped one around herself. She lay another one around Razeen's shoulders so he could do the same once he'd stopped driving.

The cars tore through the empty streets as the khamseen hit. The series of gates slid open and the cars sped up into the palace. The trees were bent double and sand filled the air. Razeen stopped the car beside the door and quickly wrapped the scarf around him. As soon as ghostly apparitions appeared, completely swathed like mummies, Razeen called "now!" and Lucy jumped out and began to run before she stopped abruptly, stunned by the massive wall of heat that hit her. For one terrifying moment she saw nothing but the whirl of sand that robbed her mouth, nose and lungs of moisture, despite the wrapping. Then suddenly Razeen grabbed her hand and pulled her inside. The doors were banged shut and they stood coughing in the main hall. Servants bustled around them, but Razeen sent them away. "Don't rub your eyes! Come." He took her by the arm and pulled her, coughing, upstairs to his suite of rooms.

They passed no one. Everywhere was empty, people having retreated to their homes and lodgings within and without the palace to make sure they were secure. There was none of the usual sounds of people, chatter, office equipment, phones ringing, only the horrible keening of the wind as it battered and glanced off every surface. Sand blew under doors and through the narrow gaps in the shutters of the window. Everywhere, the desert was threatening to overtake the city. Lucy looked down, blinking as she tried to clear her eyes. No tears emerged, despite the irritation, because the air was so dry.

Once inside the apartment, Razeen led her to the bathroom, unwound her scarf and filled the basin with water. "Here, splash your face."

She plunged her face into the running water and opened her eyes under it, allowing the water to drain out the fine grains of sand that had settled on her eyes and skin. She stood up and pushed her wet hair from her face.

"You okay?"

She shook her head. "I've never, in my life, seen anything like that before."

"It's not something anyone gets used to, not even the locals find it easy to cope with. And it can last many days, up to fifty. But not this time. Everything stops for the khamseen."

And Lucy's heart nearly did, too. He stood before her, the scarf roughly pulled around his neck, his shirt gaping with his exertions, sweat slicking his neck and body despite the dry heat, his eyes intense and reddened by the sand. She swallowed. "Everything?"

"Nearly everything."

She took a step toward him. "Thank you, Razeen. Thank you for taking me to Maia. You must have thought it stupid, but—"

He placed a finger against her lips. "Not stupid. Not stupid at all." He leaned forward and touched her lips with his own. It was a brief kiss, hardly a kiss, but it was enough to make Lucy lose her train of thought. He stepped back abruptly. "I shouldn't have done that. I'm sorry, I—"

"Razeen, we made love in the desert, we've made love at the Lodge. You *may* kiss me."

"It's not the same now."

She frowned and shook her head in confusion. "What do you mean?" He turned away and pushed his fingers through his hair. Her hand reached out and bunched the loose material of his scarf, trying to make him face her. He looked down at her then and tucked a stray strand of wet hair behind her ear, his gaze shifting from the hair to her cheeks, jaw and eyes. She saw something in his eyes she'd never seen before. "*What* are you saying?" she repeated softly but with an urgency she saw he registered.

"I knew I shouldn't have kissed you."

She frowned and pulled away. "You regret it?"

He didn't speak for a few moments. "Only because it's not fair on you."

She frowned, puzzled. "We've made love before. What's changed?"

"I saw how much it hurt you to see your sister there. You believe you've lost her. I don't want to lead you to believe I can offer you anything other than now."

"I know that, Razeen. I…" She knew that he was being fair, that he'd never promised her anything more than a few weeks together, but somehow things had changed. But, while the thought of leaving Razeen had suddenly become more painful, the thought of *not* having him in this moment was worse. "I also need to leave at the end of the week when Alex returns. I've found my sister; it won't take me long to write a report for you on the diving resort—if you still want it. There's nothing to keep me here any longer." She paused and bit her lip as she watched his face intently. "Is there?"

He shook his head. "No. I can't offer you anything more."

She frowned, wanting, more than anything to know why he couldn't, but unable to ask. She drew in a long, dry breath. "Then let's take what we have. Now. Forget everything else. There's just us: a man and a woman." Outside the wind howled and the wooden shutters rattled.

He nodded. "Just a man and a woman."

She lifted her hand to his lips. "A woman who would like to be kissed again."

No smile drifted across his face, no lightness lit his eyes, he just dipped his face to hers and pressed his lips to hers. She closed her eyes the better to feel the caress of his lips. Time slowed and every sensuous caress, every small movement of his lips against hers was felt more fully than anything that had gone before. Too soon, he pulled away.

He took her by the hand and led her to the bathroom where he turned on the taps of a huge bath. He slowly undid her abaya and slipped it off her body, shedding the fine sand that clung to ever fiber of every surface. Then he unbuttoned her shirt until it hung open loosely. He slid his finger down, tracing an unknown line over her cleavage and down to her stomach where his finger hooked into her skirt. His hand trailed around to the back fastening as he brought her to him and kissed her once more. This time there was a sense of rising passion in his kiss. He pulled away her skirt and it fell around her ankles—she hadn't even noticed he'd undone it—and she stood only in her bra and panties. He moved his hands over her body appreciatively, in a smooth caress.

"My turn."

With trembling fingers she undid the fastenings on his robe, shirt and trousers and pushed them away. He stepped out of his clothes and she slumped against him, weak with need, her forehead pressed against his chest as she inhaled him. She swept her hands over the muscled contours of his body before coming to rest on his stomach, her fingers smoothing the hairs that trailed down into his shorts. She kissed his skin, tasting the sandy-salty texture, and felt his body tremble with desire. He lifted her in his arms. She wrapped her legs around him and he stepped into the bath.

She gasped in relief as the water slid around her body and she lay back. It was as deep as a pool and she floated away, anchored by his hands around her ankles. Her hair snaked out behind her and she dipped her head back under water, feeling immense relief, not just at the shedding of sand and dust, but also at the return to what she felt to be her natural element.

But she only had a minute to enjoy the sensation before he pulled her to him and their sexes—both covered with underwear—bumped gently against each other. She wrapped her legs around him and brought her mouth to his in a kiss that was long and slow and made her forget everything else but the heat that pounded through her veins.

Too soon he pushed her away. Trembling, she stood before him as he pushed her panties down. He kissed her stomach before turning her around and unhooking her bra. Then he trailed his hands down her back, over her bottom and she closed her eyes as his hands slipped around to the front, caressing her sex, finding that place where she needed to be touched and further, down to the place that was moist and waiting.

Her legs shook as he moved his fingers over her, lingering when she gasped. With his other hand he gripped her waist and pulled her down to him. Somehow he'd taken off his shorts and he was hard under her bottom. She shifted slightly and he pushed both her legs wider, allowing his hand greater access. She continued to lift her hips, moving her bottom along his shaft, feeling his tension mount along with hers. Then he suddenly stopped.

She lay back against his chest, turned her face toward him and kissed his neck. "Don't stop."

"I want to see you, Lucy. I want to pleasure you, but I also want to make love to you. And I want you to be safe."

She turned and he held her firmly under her bottom as he lifted her out of the water and laid her gently along one of the deep, shallow steps that lined the bath. His hips were level with hers and he leaned over her body, his gaze raking its length before kissing her neck, her breasts, her stomach and her sex. Slowly he pushed open her legs, raking his fingernails up the length of her long, slender legs, tracing the tan lines left by her bikini, leading his finger to a place that was moist and ready for him. She shifted her hips, angling them, showing him her need for him.

He smiled and kissed her once more, dominating her mouth with his own. She helped him pull on the condom and caressed him until he could wait no longer and he pushed deep inside her. She cried out as she came in an explosive climax, her flesh pulsating around him, massaging him, urging him to lose himself inside her. But he didn't. He kept up a long, slow rhythm that quickly took her to the edge of a second climax. But only to the edge because he made sure he controlled them both. Only when the time was right did he release them both into an oblivion of bliss.

The first thing she noticed when she awoke was the silence. And when she opened her eyes, she saw the peculiar light had disappeared giving way to the inky black of night.

Automatically she reached for the compass and rolled out of bed—she vaguely recalled Razeen carrying her there at some point in the night—and gazed out at the lights of the city and harbor. She examined the compass, only just visible in the dim light. It was still broken. Lucy waited for the panic to begin. But it didn't come. Strange. She placed it back on the table and surveyed the city once more.

Darkness had fallen over the city. The differences in color between the city, the land and the sea were no longer there. Only the shapes remained, mused Lucy. The sea was flat and whispering, the city angular, jumbled, and subdued in the post-storm lull. She turned away from the window and glanced across at Razeen who was watching her.

"What's on your mind?"

"Why would you think anything is?"

"The way you are standing at the window, rubbing your arms as if you're cold on this hot night. The way your brow is slightly furrowed. What are you thinking about?"

She shrugged. "I'm just looking at the city and the sea, thinking…" She pursed her lips quickly, suddenly realizing she couldn't tell him what she was thinking. Because how could she tell him that it had changed in her eyes, that *he* had changed in her eyes. How could she tell him that she didn't need the compass any more? You didn't need to find out where you were when you weren't lost.

"Thinking?"

She shrugged as she tried to think of anything other than the deep pounding of her heart that contained so much for the man who'd found her and given her bearings to her. "How beautiful it is."

He frowned as if realizing he'd been fobbed off with a half-truth.

"And of Maia," she added quickly, needing to change the subject. "And of what a fool I've been, dragging you into this, wasting your time. I'm sorry, Razeen. But I'm also incredibly grateful."

"Come here."

"Another order from His Majesty?"

"Yes."

She walked over to him—trying to contain a smile at his expression of pure lust—and stood beside the bed. His hand reached out and snuck around her bottom and pulled her closer to him.

"Grateful, you say?"

"Yes," she said suspiciously.

"Exactly how grateful?" A sly grin rested on his lips.

She grinned back. "Extremely."

"And how do you intend to express this gratitude? I'm not sure verbal acknowledgement is adequate."

She pretended to look concerned. "What do you suggest?"

Suddenly he'd slipped both hands around her body and she was pulled down flat on top of him. She wriggled against his hardening form. She shifted up his body a little until he was also touching her where she needed to be touched.

"I'll leave that up to you. Anything come to mind yet?"

He pulled her legs either side of his body until she was sitting on top of him.

"Umm. I'm not sure. Oh look, I can see out of the window easier from this height. I can see the mosque up on the hill and the lights around the—"

He sat up and stole the rest of her words with a kiss. "Focus, Lucy."

"I am."

"On me."

She laughed.

"And how best might I do that?"

"I suggest you get comfortable first."

She lifted herself up as if to move away and dipped her head to one side as if in confusion. "I'm not sure if this is a good idea."

"Sit down, Lucy. You're not going anywhere."

She fluttered her eyelashes at him. "Well, you *are* the King, I suppose." And she sat, taking him inside her with one long, smooth movement.

He gasped. "Lucy!" Her name rushed from his lips as he pushed her off. He reached behind him and grabbed a packet. "Now, where were you?"

She narrowed her gaze. "Let's see if I can remember." She moved her body.

"Here?" She sat close. "Or—"

He lifted her up by the waist and she slipped back over him. "Is this what you wished for, Your Majesty?" He nodded. She moved up slightly and then down, trying to contain her own reactions to the slide of him inside her, stimulating her, threatening her control. "And this?"

He growled, his gaze narrowed. She pushed her hands against his arms, gripping his muscles that flexed under her touch. She adored his strength, his manliness. It reflected the inner man: so capable, strong...so many things, but no contradictions. This was a man she trusted. At the thought, the sensations broke through her control and she came, crying out his name into the night. He turned her over and drove into her with the same powerful need, his cry losing itself into her mouth as he claimed it with his own.

Something had happened. Lucy could see it in Razeen's eyes. He smiled briefly before finishing his coffee.

"It seems I have official visitors later today, Lucy. I'll be busy this evening. Would you like me to arrange a guide for you?"

She frowned, hurt by his cool words. Was that it? Had their brief time together already come to an end?

"No. Thank you, but no. I have plans this morning. Aakifah, the woman I met in the market, left word. She asked me to call in to see her before I left."

"I see." A long silence fell. "You look lost in thought," Razeen continued. "Care to tell me what's on your mind?"

She met his gaze directly. "Only if you do." He looked away first. "No," she continued, "forget that. I *will* tell you what I'm thinking. I'm thinking of you." She frowned and took a deep breath, more a sigh as the air hitched high in her lungs, as if searching for elusive oxygen. "I was thinking that my first impressions of you on the beach that night haven't changed at all." Again the pause, and again she filled it. "You are as you first appear."

He closed his eyes briefly. "That is one thing then, I'm glad of. That I haven't deceived you in any of my actions, or words."

She frowned, confused. "No. Why would you? No, what I meant was that you, Your Majesty, are someone to be trusted."

The silence was even heavier than before. "I think you don't know me, Lucy."

"Not well, admittedly. But from everything you do, and from everything I sense, I know you can be trusted."

He shook his head, rose from the breakfast table and absently scooped up some papers from an adjoining table. Anger filled her. She loved him.

She'd realized that in the middle of the night. But she also realized that he didn't love her. But the hell with it, he *would* listen to her.

She stood in front of him and dipped her head so she could see his face. "Did you hear me, Razeen? I trust you."

"You, Lucy, are naïve."

"You're kidding me. I've been around the world, in all sorts of company, I've probably led a less sheltered life than you have."

"You don't know the ways of the world like I do."

"Yes I do," she frowned. "What is it you're trying to tell me?"

"Just that," he twisted round as if impatient with the words he was about to utter, "you can't trust me." He gazed at her full and long. "So don't."

She stepped away as if struck. "What's the matter?" She shook her head in disbelief. "Why does me trusting you scare you?"

He gripped her arms. "You said you'd be here for a few more days only. Do I understand you correctly when you say you want no more than that?"

"Why? Do you think I'm going to start making demands on you? Razeen, I don't stay in one place. It's not me. I'm just saying I trust you, not that I want to marry you." She flung off his hands. "Look, forget I ever said anything. Forget last night too, while you're at it. It was obviously a mistake."

The blood-red sun was beginning to fill the sky behind him, making his face even darker, more unreadable than before. "I'm sorry, Lucy. You misunderstand. It was not a mistake, from my point of view. It's just that I don't wish to see you hurt."

"You flatter yourself. You give yourself too much power. I can look after myself. Now, if you'll excuse me, I'll get ready to go out. If that's all right with you, that is? I have Your Majesty's permission?"

"Of course you may go. Providing you take someone—"

Lucy didn't hear his last words. The slam of the door behind her swallowed them up. It didn't matter. He had no power over her as a King or a lover. She'd do as she damn well pleased. Just as she always did. That was what life was all about, wasn't it? Experience, fun, moving on. Not being dictated to by anyone.

As she walked through the gardens, now being hosed down to remove the dust and sand that had settled everywhere, a residue of the storm, her mind rested on Maia and doubt swept through her. Maia had always been more adamant than her about moving on, taking life lightly, but she'd changed. Part of Lucy felt betrayed and yet part of her felt doubtful now. Especially now she realized the depth of her feelings for Razeen. Not that they made any difference to her future. Maia might be able to ignore her past but Lucy couldn't ignore hers.

There were people everywhere after the storm, cleaning out the sand, tidying up. As Lucy passed by the gardens, sprays of water filled the air, casting rainbows in the sunshine. The interior of the palace was also being given the same treatment. Everyone was busy brushing out the sand that had crept into every corner, that had found its way through all the city's inadequate defenses: defenses which were powerless against such a force of nature.

Outside the palace, Aakifah was waiting for her and the two embraced as if they were long-lost friends and walked off down the street, toward Aakifah's home.

"Everyone's real busy today. What's going on? Just the usual clean up?"

"It is the visit of Her Royal Highness

Princess Neelam. I have a friend in the palace. Apparently they're all surprised by the visit. She should have arrived next week."

"I've heard of her. Isn't her father a big landowner?"

"Yes, a very important man. A very fine family."

"That's a lot of trouble to go to for someone calling in."

"It is not just someone."

"Who, then?"

"Princess Neelam is to be King Razeen's fiancee. It is expected their engagement will be announced this weekend."

CHAPTER TEN

Engaged! Lucy doubled up, gasping, as if all the air had been punched out of her.

"Lucy! What is the matter?"

Lucy eased herself upright, fighting for breath and fighting the images that raced through her brain: of Razeen laughing with her, making love to her, talking to her of anything but the fact that he was engaged to be married. She hadn't realized until that moment just how much she felt for him, how much she really had trusted him. *That* was a joke. No wonder he'd been so angry with her comments. He knew he wasn't to be trusted and he hadn't even bothered to tell her why.

"I'm fine, I think. Must be the heat. How about we stop for a moment." She glanced around and saw they were outside a coffee shop. "I'll buy us some coffees, yes?" From the excited light in Aakifah's eyes, Lucy realized her new friend had no money for such luxuries. "Perhaps you could order for us? Coffee and how about some date cake?"

They sat at a rough bench and drank and ate while watching the people go about their business: some already back on the street selling their goods, but most still cleaning up after the storm. Lucy half-listened to Aakifah's talk of her friends and TV shows but Lucy's thoughts were dominated by Razeen and his betrayal. Yet, *not* his betrayal, she realized. He'd always been clear they would be together for only two weeks. The fact it had turned into one week appeared to have surprised even him.

"Lucy, what is the matter? You do not hear what I am saying."

Lucy drew in a deep breath. "I'm sorry. Tell me again. Why does your mother want to see me?"

"She said I should not tell you. That you seeing, is the best. No, I was talking about the Princess who will soon be Queen. We are all very excited. She is of the best noble family."

Lucy's heart sank. "What's she like?" She tried to keep her voice neutral, tried not to express the aching jealousy that surged within her.

"Very beautiful of course. She has large—"

"No," Lucy interrupted, trying to contain her irritation at what Aakifah had just said. "What's she like as a person?"

Aakifah shrugged. "We know only what she looks like. People like us know little about the rich people in our country."

"Does she do good works? Does she help people?"

"Oh no, that is not her job. All we know is that she is a very suitable wife for the King, it will be very good for the country."

"In what way will a woman who keeps herself to herself be good for the country?"

"It is about tradition, connections. Of course she will not be of real help in other ways."

Anger blazed inside, burning away the hurt and jealousy. She remembered the times when Razeen had appeared in public—so distant from his people, so different to the real Razeen. He'd said that *that* was what was expected, that *that* was what his country needed. But how could that be so, when people like Aakifah and her family needed more practical help than watching their royal family uphold tradition?

"Of course." Lucy finished her coffee. "Shall we go?"

Aakifah helped Lucy step over some building rubble and led her to a narrow doorway in an old stone wall. Lucy followed Aakifah through the open door and found herself in a small, dark room, crammed with women. Lucy recognized Aakifah's mother who smiled at her and spoke a stream of Arabic.

"My mother offers you a thousand thanks for coming."

"My pleasure. I'm very pleased to see her again."

She sat where indicated and returned the mother's eager nods of welcome. "Perhaps you could tell your mother that I hope she is well?"

Aakifah nodded and was greeted by a barrage of foreign words from her mother. She nodded a few times before turning to Lucy. "My mother thanks you and says that she'd asked you to come because of my little sister." Aakifah pursed her lips together grimly. "She is the youngest of eight of us but my mother insisted she breast feed her. But my mother hasn't been well. She's been very tired and my sister is pale. She has the white sickness."

"The what?"

"I don't know what you call it but a few years ago a doctor who was treating my cousin for it said there were tablets you could buy overseas. Could you help us get some please?" Suddenly everyone was quiet; the tension in the room was palpable. In the gloom, Aakifah's eyes shone. "She just lies there: she doesn't play, she can't concentrate. We are so worried she will become like my cousin, whose parents could not afford the treatment."

"Let me see her."

Lucy was no doctor but a quick check of the little girl made her realize the child was suffering from extreme anemia.

"You need to get her to a doctor."

"We cannot afford the doctor. My mother said I should ask you what to do. I'm sorry, but we didn't know what else to do."

"That's okay. You did the right thing. I'll get the palace doctor to call. It looks like anemia to me, but the doctor will need to confirm before we start treatment. What does she eat?"

It only took Lucy a short while to identify the problem. Their diet was seriously deficient in iron. She knew from her studies that the bread, which was their main staple food, could be contributing to their inability to absorb iron and the children were all breastfed from mothers who were often lacking iron themselves.

"I will ask at the palace and arrange for a doctor to come to you."

"But we can't pay."

"Luckily, I can." She put her hand on her friend's arm. "No, really. I'm happy to help. Don't worry. And I'll see what else can be done to help you and other girls like your sister. Leave it with me."

Lucy arrived back at the palace and immediately tried to see Razeen.

"He's not available." The assistant was polite but firm, different to the day before. Lucy suddenly realized just how much things had changed.

"I'll wait." She smiled, equally firmly, at the assistant and sat outside his suite of offices.

The assistant crossed her arms. "That will not be convenient. His Majesty will not be able to receive you today. He has other matters to deal with."

Lucy held the woman's stern gaze. "These other matters must have been brought forward. He wasn't expecting them until next week."

Did she imagine it or did the woman

look surprised at Lucy's knowledge? The woman cleared her throat. "Indeed, Princess Neelam decided to surprise His Majesty."

"I'm sure she's done that." Lucy looked impatiently over the woman's shoulder. "I'll wait."

And she did. The hours ticked by but by then Lucy's heels had dug in and she refused to move on principle. The anger sparked at the news of Razeen's betrothal had been fanned by the revelation of the needless suffering being endured by Aakifah and her family and, no doubts, thousands like them. And she held on to that anger like a talisman that would see her safely through the next few days until she could leave.

At last the door opened and a number of people emerged, but not Razeen. The doors closed again. Razeen's assistants had disappeared with the rush of people, presumably to show them out. Lucy rose and tapped at the door.

She heard a grunt that sounded vaguely encouraging and she pushed open the door. Razeen sat, his elbows on the table, his fingers steepled and pressed to his mouth in an expression of thoughtful despair.

He jumped up when he saw Lucy and moved toward her. "I was just thinking about you."

"I'm not surprised." She stepped away, keeping both her body and voice as cold and stiff as possible. "I've been sitting outside for two hours."

He stopped short of her, the smile that had hovered on his lips now gone. "I'm sorry." He paused, too long, as if he was apologizing for more than just her long wait. He cleared his throat. "I've been busy but you should have told my assistant, she'd have—"

"I did, and she didn't let me see you."

"I see." He stepped closer to her, his

eyes searching hers. "I'm glad you waited." He reached out to her but she stepped back, her mouth twisting in pain, as she tried to rein in her own desire to hold him close.

"How could you, Razeen? How could you?"

He frowned. "You heard, then."

"Of course. It would have been hard not to."

"She's waiting for me. I'm to dine with her."

They stood a stride apart from each other but the distance felt insurmountable. "You're not going before you hear me out."

"Of course. I deserve anything you care to accuse me of."

Her lip curled. "You flatter yourself that I came to talk about personal matters. They've gone. Dead. You killed them. Nothing more to be said. No, why I'm here is that I saw Aakifah today. The woman I met at the market."

He frowned. "I remember."

"Her youngest sister is suffering from anemia. She needs urgent medication."

"Then she should go to the clinic."

"The clinics are corrupt, Razeen," she shouted, allowing all the pent-up emotion she was holding close, to erupt into anger. "Don't you know that?"

"Medicine is accessible to those in need. There are laws."

"Laws that don't work."

He shook his head. "Ridiculous."

"If you or your assistants went and spoke to the people once in a while you might know that. It would cost them a month's earnings—which they don't have saved—to buy the medicine. The disease is rife—the iron in the bread they make is inaccessible because it's rich in phytates: too many phytates, no iron. The women breastfeed exclusively for too long and are only just getting by, themselves." She was shaking with rage and frustration, furious at him for so many things. Tears gathered in her eyes but she had to continue. "Aakifah's sister needs a doctor." She put a piece of paper with the address into Razeen's hand. "Urgently."

He pressed his lips together for control, but control of what—anger at her, frustration at his government—she couldn't tell. "I'll make sure she gets help."

"Thank you." She rose to go.

"Lucy, where are you going?"

She didn't turn round. "To my room."

"I'll see you later."

"No. It's over." He was beside her in a second, forcing her to turn to him. "*Razeen*, don't you understand? You wanted me to trust you. I did. But you didn't trust me with the truth, did you? You didn't ever mention you were to be married; never said anything about a fiancée visiting you within a week of our making love. Did you think it would spoil the ambience?" She couldn't prevent the bitterness creeping into her words. "Did you think I'd say 'no'? Well, I would have said 'no' because it's not fair on her; not fair on the woman who is pledging her life to you. How do you think she'd feel if she knew her fiancée-to-be had been sleeping with someone? No doubt you'll find out when she discovers our relationship. You've hardly kept it a secret."

"I deserve all you say. But you misunderstand Neelam. Of course she knows. And she thinks none the worse of me for it. Her father has three wives. She wouldn't expect me to marry more than once, but neither would she expect fidelity."

Lucy shook her head. "I don't believe that. All women want fidelity. No woman wants to share her man with anyone else."

"Is that how you feel?"

"You're twisting my words. I—"

"I want you to attend dinner." She watched as his face hardened, as he became the King once more. "You will be at dinner. You will dine with us and you will see Neelam. Perhaps *then* you will understand."

She gasped. "No, I will not."

"You *will* be there. If you're not there at eight, I will come to you, throw you over my shoulder, and take you there like the primitive man you appear to think I am."

"You wouldn't dare."

"Try me." He raised his eyebrows in an unsmiling question that she didn't answer. The air between them sizzled with anger and something else she dare not contemplate.

She turned and left the room without a further word.

* * *

Lucy slipped into the seat reserved for her in a corner of the huge dining room. Only a few people looked at her knowingly. She'd been positioned where she could watch and listen to Neelam easily and, more disconcertingly, Razeen could watch Lucy easily. She sensed Razeen had noted her arrival but he didn't meet her eyes. For the hundredth time that evening she wondered if she should have come. It wasn't Razeen's threat that made her turn up. She'd be gone in a few days and she needed to know, needed to see with her own eyes, the woman Razeen would be marrying.

And Aakifah was right. Neelam was beautiful. Large, wide eyes and a perfect oval face framed by lustrous dark hair. Lucy bit her lip and concentrated on her food. What the hell had she been thinking? Why would Razeen ever want *her* when he could have someone like Neelam: beautiful, well connected and wealthy.

Lucy sipped a spoonful of soup

and glanced around. There were no burkhas, abayas, scarves or hijabs tonight: only expensive Parisian and London fashions that showcased their wealth. The colors and cut stones sparkled in the light. She half-regretted wearing her vintage red evening dress. She'd picked it up for a song in Paris but it was good quality and it made her look like one of them. And she didn't want to look like one of them now, because it made her feel sick inside thinking of Aakifah and her family needing essential medicine while Razeen was sucked into this world of remote luxury. It wasn't him. She knew that and yet he'd been persuaded that was what was required.

She looked at Neelam once more. She was looking down, listening to the young women who sat beside her, talking of the latest fashions. Lucy felt her resentment mount at the inane chatter and then Neelam glanced up and caught her gaze. Instantly Lucy could see that Neelam knew who she was. But there was no anger, no jealousy in her eyes. Instead she nodded briefly and smiled hesitantly. Neelam's eyes were kind and they were also intelligent. Lucy returned the smile awkwardly and turned away first. She felt awful, as if she'd betrayed Neelam. But, more than that, she was angry with Razeen for putting her in this position.

Suddenly she was aware of Razeen's eyes upon her. She didn't meet them but focused on her dinner and toyed with her food. She'd never been less hungry and yet the food was sumptuous. Luckily the person she sat next to was more interested in her other companions and she was left to her own devices. She had no option but to listen to Neelam's friends' chatter while Neelam herself remained silent.

By the end of the first course, Lucy just hoped Neelam wasn't like her friends because if she was, there would be no help for those people of Sitra who needed it. She glanced angrily at Razeen. He sipped his water and met her gaze levelly. It was as if he read her thoughts. In which case why the hell didn't he understand that Neelam might be of the correct elite to satisfy his traditional advisors but she was too young, too distant and, if her friends were anything to go by, too shallow to help him bring his country into the modern day?

Lucy couldn't take any more and, despite a warning glance from Razeen, she rose and quickly slipped away.

Lucy didn't even have the energy to undress. She lay on her bed listening to the silence that had hung over the old domestic wing of the palace all evening. She listened to the water running through the rills and channels outside in the garden and wondered how the hell her world had shattered quite so spectacularly in the space of one week.

It was as if the winds of the khamseen had whisked through her life disabling first the fixed compass point of Maia, from whom she'd always been able to work out her bearings. And, second, cracking open the strength on which she'd always relied, to reveal a vulnerability, a heart, that had been trampled on by a man who'd proclaimed himself to be someone she could trust. He may have been right about trusting him with her life, with anything, other than her heart that he'd taken and crushed.

She pushed down the frothy layers of her red dress and turned onto her side to look out into the night sky and was suddenly aware of another sound above the trickle of water. It was the sound of feet walking toward her room. She froze. No servants passed these guest quarters. She glanced at the door and was relieved to remember she'd locked it. There was a knock but she didn't answer. She lay in the warm, heated dark and listened to her heart pound, wanting, desperately wanting the man she knew to be the other side but knowing if she answered the door, she'd lose the strength she needed to carry on.

She heard the footsteps retreat. She lay back and waited for her heart to steady. She took deep breaths and tried to keep her mind on track. Her bags were packed. Alex had responded to her text and luckily his boat would dock first thing in the morning. She'd be on it before breakfast. They'd be sailing later that night.

Still her heart pounded. She rose from the bed, poured herself a glass of water and pushed open the French doors to let in the cooler night air. It was then that she saw him coming toward her.

"What the hell are you doing? Can't I have any privacy?"

"No." He continued walking up to her.

She slapped her hand against his chest. "Go away Razeen, I don't want you here."

He ignored her and grabbed her hands. "And what did you think of the beautiful Neelam?"

"You're mad if you ever think she'll help you move this country forward. You're crazy. She's not what you need."

"Then who is?"

She shook her head. "Go away, Razeen."

She couldn't see his expression in the starlight but she sensed he was frustrated and angry.

"I want you to come with me. I have something to show you." It was as if she'd never spoken.

"Do I have a choice?"

"At last you are understanding the power of the sheikh," he said facetiously. "This way."

He led her through darkened halls to a corner of his private quarters she'd not visited before. He opened the door for her to enter and closed it behind them both. She was momentarily swallowed up in darkness until Razeen switched on a small lamp. Despite the anger she was awed. She turned around on the spot, her gaze shifting from the priceless artworks on the walls to the intricately worked ceiling. While it was as richly decorated as the rest of the palace, it was on a smaller, more intimate scale. It wasn't a place to impress people, it was a place to appreciate its treasures.

"It's beautiful." Lucy's voice was hushed as she walked around the bijoux room.

"It was my mother's. She was English."

Razeen became more of a stranger to her with each passing hour. She realized she knew nothing about him. She sighed and looked down at the priceless rug, suddenly feeling defeated. "I thought your parents were both from Sitra."

"No. My father was educated at Eton and Oxford and fell in love with a society beauty."

There was a sadness behind Razeen's even tone that made her look up. "What happened?"

"She had two children—my brother and me—and died alone and unhappy. She was never accepted into Sitra and my father grew to resent that. He lost a lot of support over it. He increasingly turned his back on the West, kept Sitra isolated. They both grew bitter. It was not a happy place to grow up in. My mother was deeply unhappy."

"Why didn't she return to England?"

"Because that would have been even worse for my father. It would have brought great shame to him and to the kingdom. She sacrificed her happiness for my brother's future as King."

"Not your future."

"No, not mine. It was always about the future of Sitra and so, it was always about my brother."

She walked over to a table upon which photographs were placed. She picked one up. "She was beautiful." She replaced the photograph and picked up another, of Razeen and his brother. "And you were very cute."

"Just 'were'?" She turned to find him behind her, a ghost of a smile resting on his lips.

"Searching for compliments?"

There was no humor in his eyes now. "Lucy, do you see what I'm trying to tell you? This is no place for a western woman. There can be no future for us."

She replaced the photograph carefully on the table. "Your mother and father made mistakes. They were different people to us. You're right but for the wrong reasons. There is no future for us because I'll be leaving in the morning."

"I'm sorry, Lucy. It was never meant to be this way." He touched her cheek with his fingertips so gently, that all resolve disintegrated.

She swallowed as she dropped her gaze to his lips. She licked her own. "*How* was it meant to be?"

"You, passing through; me, a brief reprieve before I was dragged down by duty."

She raised her eyes to his and at the sight of the pain that dwelled there, she placed her hand on his chest, above his heart. "But that's surely what's still happening. I'm leaving tomorrow morning; you're going to be doing your duty."

"Yes, you're right. That is still what's happening on the surface. But inside?" He curled his fingers under her chin and swept his thumb over her bottom lip. "I knew there was a risk I might end up wanting something—someone—I could never have, and that was a risk I was prepared to take. But I never wanted to hurt you."

She dropped her gaze and he took the step across the space between them and pressed her head against his chest, his arms cradling her body as he kissed the top of her hair.

"And I think I have. I'm so sorry, Lucy."

She closed her eyes as she breathed him in, her lips grazing his neck. "Forget about me. You can't marry her, Razeen. She's not best for this country; she's not best for you."

"Now *there* you are at great variance to all my advisers."

"Then dismiss them. They're wrong."

He shook his head and pulled away from her. "No, they're not. They know Sitra and they know the Sitran people. My country needs reform and my people demand a traditional King."

"Have you asked your people what they want? Have you? Or is it just a few advisors you're relying on. Razeen, you need to get out there amongst your people, find out what's happening, discover what they want. Look at my sister, she's going to make a huge difference to the people she lives with. You think they won't appreciate that? Look at me," she slammed her fist into her chest, repeatedly, trying to control the passion that threatened to overflow. "Look at me, look at how the women in the market have accepted me. Doesn't that count for more than being of the right blood?"

"I wish it were that simple."

"It is, Razeen, it is."

"You don't understand, Lucy. You've been here a week and you think you know the situation better than me? Than my advisers? Come on, even you cannot be that naive."

She drew her arms defensively in front of her, suddenly feeling cold. "Well, if you've quite finished I'll go back to bed. I've an early morning start." She stepped awkwardly away and walked briskly to the door.

"I'm sorry—"

She held up her hand to stop him from speaking any further. She couldn't turn to him, couldn't face him. "Don't. Just let me go."

"I cannot make my own choices any more, my life is not my own."

"I seem to remember you telling me that it wasn't madness for Maia to freely choose where she wished to be."

"But I am *not* free to choose. You must understand."

"I can't see it makes much difference whether I understand or not." She turned to face him, needing to know. "But tell me, Razeen, if you were free, what, or who would you choose?"

The silence lay heavy between them.

Razeen didn't speak, only looked at her with an expression she couldn't read.

"I see." She turned away.

"I'm sorry, Lucy, that things can't be different."

The slam of the door echoed through the sleeping palace and Razeen closed his eyes as the pain washed through him. There was no doubt in his mind that they had no future together. There were so many reasons he couldn't be with Lucy. No responsible man would have done otherwise. It was not only necessary for the future of the kingdom but he couldn't go back on the word he'd given to his future wife and her family.

And, he thought as he picked up the photo of his mother, it was necessary for Lucy's future happiness. He knew what his mother's life had become; he knew how unhappy she'd been. And he also knew how much his parents had been in love to begin with. He picked up another photo of them on their wedding day. His father was unrecognizable: his face bright and happy. There was nothing to indicate the tyrant he would become. Even love couldn't withstand such pressure.

He replaced the photos but continued to stare at the photograph of his mother, the details obscured under the hollow glare of the lamp. His eyes stung as he stared unblinking at the photo. But he'd ceased to see his mother and saw, instead, Lucy's face—tense and hurt. Without taking his eyes from the photo he groped for the light switch and turned it off. His mother's face was no longer visible: but Lucy's face haunted him still.

CHAPTER ELEVEN

Five months later…

Lucy lay back on the sun lounger and sighed. She'd spent all morning in the boat's galley preparing dinner and it felt good to have the sun's rays on her body again. She closed her eyes and flipped her sunglasses onto her nose.

A shadow fell over her body. She didn't bother opening her eyes; it could only be Alex. The others were all eating.

"Hey, you're in my sun."

"You'll be getting plenty of sun soon."

"I'll be covered from head to foot with an abaya and my tan will suffer."

"Yes, I suppose so. Hadn't thought of

it like that." He paused, hesitant, and Lucy opened her eyes and turned to him.

"What's up? Want to persuade me to stay?"

He grinned. "Now, I know that wouldn't work. You'll be with your sister for the birth of her child come hell or high water."

"Yep. And I want to get there a few days early. She's not due for another week but I don't want to miss out. I figure I'll hang around for a while after the birth to help out and then I'll leave."

"There's always a job here, if you want one."

"You're too good to me. You've found a replacement chef now. You don't need me."

"I could have two cooks. Sounds good to me."

"You don't *need* two. Don't worry about me. I'll be fine. There's always work in the Caribbean. I'll try there first."

"You may want to stay in Sitra."

She looked out across the sea she loved so much for its ever-changing moods and constant movement. "No, I won't. I never stay long in one place. I don't do 'permanent.'"

"I thought Razeen might have changed your mind on that point."

"He's not interested. I don't know why you think he is. Anyway, he has nothing to do with my reason for returning. I'm there for Maia and that's all."

"He *is* interested, Lucy. Of course he is."

"No 'of course' about it."

"He told me."

Her head snapped round. "What?"

"Razeen is my friend, Lucy, we stay in touch. Particularly after the debacle of the wedding." He paused. "Do you want to know what happened?"

"No." She gnawed the inside of her lip to hide her uncertainty. "I know the bare essentials, that's quite enough."

"Shame."

There was a long pause while Alex walked to the mast and yanked a knot a bit tighter. Lucy tried to keep her curiosity tamped down. She fidgeted with her hands, crossed and uncrossed her ankles and then took a deep breath knowing that Alex wasn't going to go away until she'd asked.

"I shouldn't think there's much more to be said."

"Shouldn't think so," he agreed.

"I know the marriage didn't happen. But as to why? Who knows?" Again a teasing silence. "Alex?"

"I might know."

"Damn it, Alex, tell me. What happened? Who called it off? Was it Razeen?" She knew it had to have been. After all, he *was* the one with the power *and* the one who had no love for his fiancée.

Alex shook his head. "No, it wasn't

Razeen."

Lucy sat bolt upright, her sunglasses falling to the wooden deck with a clatter.

"What?"

"His fiancée called it off. Seems she was more enamored with a life outside Sitra than one in it. She's in Paris now, studying at the Sorbonne."

"He'd have gone through with it then." The words emerged on a rush of exhaled air. Disappointment bit deep. She'd believed he'd listened to her and called it off. But he hadn't. It had been the shy and intelligent girl who'd made the break.

"Yes, he'd have gone through with it. He's very serious about his responsibilities. You should know that."

"Yes," she chewed her lip and glanced away. "I do."

She made herself lie back. Alex walked over to the railing and peered out at the horizon with narrowed eyes.

There was only the lapping of the water against the boat and the occasional shout and background chatter of the crew eating lunch in the cabin to break the lengthening silence.

"I thought you two were pretty well suited, you know."

"Did you?" She tried to sound unconcerned.

"Yeah, I reckon you could have made a good go of it together."

"Umm. Obviously he didn't share that view."

"What makes you say that?"

She sat up and sighed. "Oh, I don't know. Perhaps the way he was determined to marry someone else?"

"Well, he didn't."

"Not through his own choice. And then there's the fact that, after his marriage didn't happen, he chose not to contact me. You don't have to be Sherlock Holmes to make a reasonable deduction that he's not interested in me."

"Or that he believes any advance from him wouldn't be welcome. And then there's his family history. Come on, Luce, you know what happened to his mother. He adored her and she just retreated, left him to it because she couldn't handle life in Sitra. He's terrified if he marries someone from outside his country, the same thing would happen. And he can't do that to someone he loves."

"Someone he loves..." she repeated faintly.

"Look, all I'm saying is, give him a chance. When you get to Sitra and see him—"

"I won't be seeing him. Maia's made arrangements for me to stay in an apartment in the city. I won't be going anywhere near the palace. He doesn't even know I'm going to Sitra."

"When you see him," Alex continued as if he hadn't been interrupted, "give him a chance."

"I *gave* him a chance, Alex," she said quietly, "and he didn't take it. He doesn't want me."

"I don't believe that."

"Perhaps I should rephrase it. He might want me—I don't know—but he won't have me. End of story."

"Not yet it's not." Alex grinned and walked back inside the cabin.

* * *

The heat hit Lucy like a wall as she left the airport terminal and she was thankful she'd bought a lightweight abaya and nijab. With her hair hidden, and her tan and kohled eyes, she hoped she'd fit in and, from the way no one was looking at her, she did.

As she walked toward the small taxi rank she passed a luxurious car whose driver stood, hands on hips, scanning the people leaving the flight with great care. She recognized him; he was from the palace. She put her head down and kept on walking. The thought that Razeen might have been alerted to her return and had sent the driver to collect her, briefly flashed through her mind. But she kept on walking. He'd made it clear he didn't want her so why on earth would he have sent someone for her?

She jumped into a taxicab and gave the driver the address in the city she'd been given. Within ten minutes they were crawling through the busy, closely built old quarter. He parked outside one of the merchants' houses and pointed. After collecting the key from the family who both lived and worked in the shop downstairs she went up the well-worn steps to the first-floor apartment.

It was surprisingly beautiful—the furniture was obviously expensive—and great thought had been given to every detail: from the fully stocked refrigerator and cupboards, to the bed, which was made up in snowy white linen. She trailed her hand along the highly polished table and opened the windows wide.

The views were amazing. The city spread out before her, its roofs, arched windows and peeling walls all soft ochre and terra cotta, like so many daubs of water color paint on paper. Beyond the tumble of buildings lay the bay. She felt if she reached out she'd touch the blue, and feel the cool water. Just seeing the sea again made her feel more comfortable. The sound of the muezzin calling the faithful to prayer echoed over the city and the spicy aroma of coffee wafted up from the cafe below. It was perfect. And she always had to share perfect.

She reached for her phone and found a message from Maia. All was well and she'd be arriving in the city later the next day. Lucy softly blew out a tense breath. She was nervous for Maia but was reassured by her breezy message.

And a day to herself would give her a chance to visit Aakifah and her family. Lucy had received one brief, formal letter from Aakifah letting her know that a doctor had called and given them the medicine her sister needed. Not only that, but clinics had been set up around the city where treatment was provided free and research was being conducted into some of the more common ailments. Lucy hadn't needed a letter from Aakifah to know this would happen. She knew Razeen wouldn't let her down; she knew he wanted to do the absolute best for his people, no matter what the personal cost.

She rubbed her chest with the heel of her hand. It hurt. No matter what she told Alex, Razeen's rejection of her hurt bad. Even overseas he'd haunted her mind every minute of every day. But here, surrounded by the sights and sounds of Sitra, it was more intense.

The smell of the coffee reminded her of the taste of it on his lips; the glittering turquoise of the sea reminded her of making love to him in the surf: his body, so strong and lithe, holding her against him. She turned away from the sea. She had to get out. She swept up her bag and walked across to the door when the sound of a bell ringing loudly in the apartment stopped her in her tracks. She went down the stairs slowly and paused, before she lifted her shaking hand to the lock and opened the door wide.

A palace official bowed politely and offered a letter to her. Thanking him in her hesitant Arabic, she closed the door and opened the letter. It was a formal request to go to the palace that afternoon signed by an official she'd never heard of. She read it through again, trying to find something more in the collection of words than an invitation to the palace. What was it for? It didn't say. She screwed it up, pushed it deep in her bag meaning to throw it into the next available bin, and headed out into the bright sunlight to visit her friends. Just an official invitation, nothing personal. Just as well, she reassured herself, because she'd have run a mile. She'd be leaving in a few weeks, just as she always did. Domestic stuff wasn't her. Domestic stuff spelled...heartache. So just as well Razeen had made it clear he didn't want her.

* * *

The sun was glowing red in the sky by the time Razeen saw Lucy turn the corner, laughing with a couple of young women who were accompanying her. He felt her presence enter his body like a drug; his body recognized and welcomed her on every level, through every vein, every nerve of his body. He took a sip of his coffee and tried to look inconspicuous amongst the other cafe patrons. He wanted to watch her for as long as possible, unguarded and relaxed, just being Lucy.

She was talking ten-to-a-dozen and the women obviously adored her, no doubt unable to understand a quarter of what she was saying. But they were laughing and chatting back in Arabic, which no doubt Lucy could only barely understand, aided only by the occasional translation of one woman, presumably Aakifah.

And so they should be appreciative of her, he thought. She'd done more single-handedly for their welfare than any of his family since his grandfather. But, looking at them now, he realized two things. One, that the women didn't only appreciate Lucy, they *really* liked her. They made contact with her, their hands resting on her arms when they spoke; they moved freely before her, laughing and joking as if she were an old friend. He realized with a start that she was accessible to them in a way that his family had never been to the people. The other thing that struck him forcibly was that the regard went both ways. Lucy looked totally at home with them, despite the language barrier.

He frowned and turned away, replacing his coffee cup carefully on the table. As soon as Lucy had left he realized she had been right and his advisors had been wrong. He needed a Queen whose heart and soul were invested in Sitra. Neelam's heart and soul yearned to leave Sitra and so he'd encouraged her to leave to follow her dreams and the wedding had been called off. But more than a passion for his country, he needed a Queen he could love. And that meant only one person. But this realization hadn't made him track down Lucy and propose to her. How could he when she clearly demonstrated, by both her lack of words and her actions, that she didn't love him?

He watched her farewell her friends and walk across the street toward him. And in that moment he knew he had to find out what she felt for him—good or bad—he *had* to know.

It wasn't until Lucy stopped beside the cafe to pluck her keys out of her bag that she saw him. Her breath nearly froze in her throat as he met her gaze and rose to meet her.

"You've been gone a long time."

"I've been with my friends from the market."

"No, Lucy, I mean you've been away from Sitra for a long time."

"I had no reason to return."

He looked thoughtful. "But now you have."

"Yes, now I have things to do here."

She paused, gripping her key in her hand. *What the hell was he doing here?*

"May I come in?"

"I guess so." She turned the key in the lock, entered the narrow hallway and immediately climbed the stairs leading to her apartment. Razeen's footsteps followed closely behind. When they emerged into the upstairs space he stopped and looked around.

"Is this satisfactory? Maia said you didn't wish to stay at the palace so I found this for you. I'm afraid it's a little small. I'd have preferred something more fitting for you, but Maia thought you'd like it and I knew you'd be safe here. The family downstairs are trustworthy."

She turned away, not wanting to see how his words affected her. It was all thanks to him. Everything—from her favorite chocolates in the refrigerator, to the newly planted window box filled with the white scented flowers she loved so much—was down to him. "It's perfect, thank you." She turned and smiled at him. "I might have known you'd arranged it."

"Of course."

"Would you like a coffee or tea?"

"I've drunk enough coffee while waiting for you."

"I bet you don't have to wait around for people very often."

"Indeed. But as you refused my invitation to come to the palace, I had no choice." He stepped closer to her, his head tilted to one side as if to see her better.

"The King who has no choice. Nothing much changes, does it?" She couldn't prevent the bitterness at his rejection from inflecting her words.

He narrowed his eyes briefly. "It seems you give me few. Perhaps I should even up the score and refine *your* choices."

Lucy bit her lip in a vain attempt to stop it trembling. "And how do you propose to do that?"

"I want you at the palace tonight."

She shook her head. "No, I can't. There's no point, Razeen. It's over. I'm only here for a short—"

"You misunderstand. There's to be a reception at the palace to mark the progress the clinic has made in six months of operation. That clinic is down to you, Lucy. You've made a difference. You should be there."

She turned away, embarrassed at her assumption that his visit had been personal. Of course it wasn't. He *was* the King after all.

"In that case, I'll come."

"Good. I'll have someone call for you at seven." He turned to leave but paused and turned back to face her once more. "You *will* be there, won't you? You won't disappear again."

"I've only just arrived."

"That means little. You come and go as you please with no thought to your responsibilities."

"I have none."

"And that's the way you like it, isn't it? I understand you've kept in contact with the clinic and they offered you a position with them."

"Yep, that's right."

"And you turned it down."

"Yes, of course. If you accept a job like that you have to commit to it."

"And commitment isn't something you do well, is it? Why is that, I wonder?"

"That's personal." Suddenly the room felt airless; she couldn't breathe. Razeen was coming closer and closer to that knot at the centre of things that, so many years ago, she'd bundled up and drawn shutters around to protect herself. *She* knew why she didn't do commitment, *Maia* knew why she didn't do commitment, but no one else must know. She couldn't risk unleashing the pain that still surged and flowed within the concrete tomb of her heart.

"And you can't bear to talk about the 'personal', can you, Lucy?" His voice rose suddenly, frustration evident in every syllable.

She waved her hand impatiently and walked over to the windows which she shoved open to their fullest extent, desperate to see the sea. But it was dark now and she couldn't see it. Her panic grew and she turned to find Razeen close beside her. "Leave it, Razeen. Please. I don't want to talk about it now."

He pushed her hair away from her face, distractedly watching it fall down her back. "I don't know what you're hiding from me, Lucy. But I'll find out."

The gentle touch of his hand and whispered words made the threat of discovery even more menacing. It was strange to stand so close to someone, to feel so much for someone, and yet have such a wide chasm exist between them. They stood facing each other, each of them breathing hard. Lucy didn't know if Razeen was going to kiss her or shout at her.

Suddenly there was a sharp rap at the door.

"Enter!"

A palace official entered the room. Razeen glared at him.

"What do you want? Can't you see I'm busy?"

The assistant appeared uncomfortable. "Your Majesty, it is not for you I am here. It is Miss Gee." He turned to her. "Miss Gee, your brother-in-law says you are to come at once. Your sister has been admitted to the emergency ward in the hospital. There's a problem."

CHAPTER TWELVE

Lucy's heart was thumping high in her chest, as she shakily grabbed her bag and strode over to the man. "What kind of problem?"

"I'm sorry, I don't know the details. I have a car outside." The man looked up at Razeen for approval. "If that's suitable, Your Majesty?"

"I'll take Miss Gee." Razeen turned round. "Lucy?"

But she was already running down the stairs.

* * *

The white walls of the brand-new hospital were easily visible against the

324

vast darkness of the desert. Razeen had assured Lucy the hospital was state of the art and staffed with well-qualified doctors, and that Maia would have the best care possible, but Lucy hardly listened. She was consumed by an overpowering sense of anger and frustration that Maia had stayed in the city of caves until her due date without having had regular check-ups. She was full of resentment that Mohammed had seduced Maia away from her life and hadn't cared for her properly. The compass moved on her chest and she grasped it and closed her eyes. Instantly the anger fell away leaving only the terror that Maia would leave her.

As Razeen brought the car to a screeching halt on the hot concrete in front of the emergency entrance, she gripped the door handle tightly, trying to quiet the shaking, but it didn't work. Grief rose up in her gut like a fiery ball.

"Are you okay?"

She shook her head, unable to speak, not knowing whether rational words would emerge or some primeval scream of loss.

"It'll be all right. Don't assume the worst. Come on."

They ran through the corridors to the operating theatre where they were met by a distraught Mohammed who was pacing outside. He turned to Lucy and hugged her instinctively before turning to Razeen to do the same. He stopped himself suddenly as he remembered he was about to hug the King. Instead he stumbled back and leaned against the wall, his face a picture of agony.

Lucy's heart sank but somehow seeing him so full of despair summoned up her own strength. "How is she?"

Mohammed appeared to have forgotten his English and, instead, uttered a stream of Arabic.

"He says she's had an emergency caesarian but she's hemorrhaging badly."

"Can you ask him what happened?"

But there was no need to. Mohammed gesticulated wildly while pouring forth a stream of words which Razeen listened to patiently, before turning to Lucy to translate.

"Apparently everything happened fast. They were on their way here—luckily Maia decided to leave earlier because you'd arrived—and she started bleeding. It seems the baby is well, but he doesn't know about Maia. He's waiting to be allowed back into the theatre."

Mohammed began pacing again, unable to keep still and Lucy leaned back against the wall, crossed her arms and watched him. In those moments of his grief she saw how much he loved Maia. It was written in every impatient, angry, distressed gesture, it was written in the tears that streamed down his face unchecked and in the words of self-recrimination over nonsensical things that Razeen translated. She understood then. Maia had always been popular, always had friends, but Lucy had never witnessed such utter devotion. And she was happy for Maia. Happy she'd found a home after so many years without one. It was a home she would never have herself.

As a doctor emerged through the swing-doors and spoke briefly to Razeen, she caught sight of Maia's face—deathly white, lively eyes closed now—and grief welled up inside her. "No, Maia, you can't damn well leave me." She shook her head and swiped at the tears that had begun to fall down her face. Suddenly Razeen's arms were around her. "She can't leave me." The words emerged as a moan from the fear and grief that lay knotted in the pit of her gut. She crossed her arms over her body as if to contain the pain. "Will she be all right?" She looked up at him. "She will, won't she?"

"They don't know yet. They're working hard. She has a postpartum hemorrhage, something to do with the placenta. But the blood isn't clotting easily so they're doing a transfusion of platelets." He put his arm around her and brought her to his side. "Don't worry, Lucy. She's in capable hands."

But Lucy did worry.

A nurse appeared and beckoned Mohammed who disappeared into the room. Lucy began to follow but Razeen stopped her.

"Leave him with her. They need each other now."

She bit her lip and turned away, knowing he was right. She leaned her forehead against the wall that divided her from Maia and wept. Razeen's arms folded around her and his warm body pressed against her back. He held his head against hers and murmured Arabic words of comfort that were incomprehensible but reassuring nevertheless. He continued to hold her and her sobs slowly calmed. Only then did he turned her around and pull her into his arms.

A doctor emerged and spoke briefly to Razeen. She saw from the relief on the doctor's face and Razeen's response that the worst was passed. "She's going to be okay, isn't she?"

"She's going to be fine. But she'll need some time to recuperate to regain her strength."

"Can I see her?"

"The doctors prefer you to wait. She needs rest at the moment." A nurse appeared behind him carrying a bundle. "Mohammed wants to stay with Maia and has asked if you could look after the baby."

Lucy stepped away, shaking her head. She couldn't do it. How could she possibly take responsibility for a baby? But the busy nurse didn't have time to talk and pushed the bundle into Lucy's arms. Lucy froze, holding the tiny bundle as if it were a time bomb. And it was, in a way. Because it ignited memories that had long been suppressed: of Lucy, barely more than a child herself, holding a small baby in her arms.

Then the baby wriggled and Lucy jumped, brought back to the present with a jolt. With one finger she tentatively pushed aside the swaddling blankets to look at the baby's face and she gasped, holding the breath for long seconds as she absorbed its tiny features: a stunning combination of Maia's perfect features and Mohammed's dark hair and nutmeg skin. The tears began again—she wasn't sure they'd ever stopped—and her arms instinctively drew the baby close. The baby opened its mouth briefly in a silent cry that quickly faded and then turned toward Lucy's chest and fell asleep. Lucy spread her hands over the soft wool of the blanket, curling around the baby's tender curves, and brought the bundle closer to her body. She dipped her head to inhale its sweet smell and knew in that moment that, despite the grief that was irrevocably intertwined with her own past, she could do this.

She looked at Razeen, who hadn't taken his eyes off her. "This has to be the quietest baby I've ever seen."

"She doesn't take after her aunt then."

"Is it a 'she'? I hadn't even thought to ask."

"Yes, it's a she. Mohammed said that Maia and he had decided on the name 'Noor.'"

"Noor," Lucy repeated. "That's beautiful."

"It means 'light' in Arabic."

"Same meaning as 'Lucy.'"

"I didn't know that." His voice was so soft, so tender that it drew her attention from the baby nestled in her arms.

"Thank you, Razeen, for being here for me. I would have gone to pieces without you."

His brown eyes were filled with sadness. "No," he pressed his lips together as if in regret. "No, not you. You're stronger than you think."

"Even the strong need help some times. Will you stay with me now?" He didn't answer immediately and she suddenly felt uncertain. "I'm sorry, I shouldn't ask. You must have so many things to do, I—"

"Of course I'll stay. The registrar says there's a room at our disposal. We can stay here the night and then Noor will be close to Maia when she's able to see her." He lifted her chin so he could see into her eyes. "Okay?"

Lucy nodded. "Definitely okay."

Razeen put his arm around her and gently guided her through the corridors to the suite.

As soon as Lucy sat on the couch, Noor awoke and opened her mouth and screamed. Lucy looked up anxiously at the nurse who'd just appeared. "What's the matter with her? Is she hurt?" The nurse laughed at Lucy's expression. Although obviously unable to understand her word for word, the nurse understood the gist and handed her the tiniest bottle of milk Lucy had ever seen.

"The nurse says she's hungry. That's all. Nothing to worry about."

Noor was soon latched on to the bottle and drinking contentedly. But that only caused another anxious thought to pop into Lucy's mind. "Will this mean she can't breastfeed from Maia?"

Razeen translated to the nurse before turning once more to Lucy. "She says, hopefully it should all be fine. There's no reason why it shouldn't be."

"This is so scary. There are so many things that might go wrong."

"And so many things that might go right," Razeen replied. The nurse said something Lucy couldn't understand. "The nurse says that you will make a good mother. You are already worried about everything."

Lucy shivered as if someone had walked over her grave.

"What's the matter, Lucy? The nurse meant it only as a compliment."

But Lucy couldn't smile, she couldn't reassure Razeen, she couldn't even look him in the eye. How could she tell him that, long ago, when she'd been far too young, she *had* been a mother— albeit briefly—a mother who hadn't been able to care for her own baby?

"Lucy?"

Lucy shook her head, her eyes fixed on Noor. "I can't imagine ever being a mother, especially not of a baby so perfect."

Razeen didn't answer but simply gazed down at Lucy and the baby, and felt the opposite. He couldn't imagine her *not* being a mother. But there was one difference to the scene he saw before him: the baby would be his and Lucy's and it would be more perfect.

* * *

"Lucy, when are you going to stop smiling that stupid, soppy grin? It's not like you."

Maia sat propped up in her own bed in the city of caves, the baby at her breast suckling contentedly.

"I thought I'd lost you." Lucy could feel the tears, which seemed to be her constant companion now, prick her eyes.

Maia reached for Lucy's hand and squeezed it. Lucy held it tight as if she'd never let it go again. "Not me, sis, I'm made of tougher stuff than that. It would take more than a baby to destroy *this* woman."

Lucy's grin grew broader, less soppy. "Yeah, well, I guess you always were the drama queen, Maia. You couldn't let something like childbirth go without a scene."

"Once a drama queen always a drama queen. I was pretty spectacular, wasn't I? I'd never seen Mohammed so shocked. I guess that means he loves me." She grinned smugly at Lucy.

"I think there's no doubt about that. He's besotted with you both. I can let you remain in your cave happy in the knowledge that you might be living in a cave but your caveman will always look after you."

Maia shook her head in mock irritation. "You're a fine one to talk. You're meant to be the practical one, Luce. What's all this I hear about you nearly fainting in Razeen's arms?"

"Had to do something to make him hold me."

"You really like him, don't you?"

"More than like. But there's no future. I don't want to settle down. Even if I did, he doesn't want me. He's stuck with the idea that I'd be unhappy here and that I wouldn't fit in, etc etc. He's so responsible, he has to do what he thinks right for both the country and for me. But," she shrugged, "that's irrelevant. Staying in one place isn't for me."

"He has to be responsible because he's King."

"And because he has to prove to himself that his father was wrong: prove that he *deserves* to be King and he *can* be trusted."

There was silence for a few moments while Maia shifted the baby to her other breast, her expression thoughtful. "And you came here believing Razeen had kidnapped me. Which, don't get me wrong, was very sweet of you but I doubt it went very far to improve Razeen's belief that he could be trusted when the woman he loves didn't trust him."

"What makes you think he loves me?"

"Even a drama queen can see he loves you. It's just you and him who can't seem to put two and two together."

"If it's true—even a little bit—I guess my suspicions about him would have thrown him more than I thought."

"Perhaps you just need to make him see how much you trust him."

"There's no point. If I show him I trust him, what then? I'll be leaving in a few weeks."

"But you love him, Lucy. Isn't that enough to make you stay?"

Lucy shook her head and shrugged her shoulders awkwardly. "No." She shook her head again. "As I say, I'll be leaving."

"Because of what happened so many years ago?"

"Yep, I guess. Still…"

Maia grabbed Lucy's hand. "Will you do something for me?"

Lucy was relieved at the change of subject. "Of course. You know I will. Anything."

"Tell Razeen what happened to you."

"That's just silly. Why? Why would you want me to do that?"

"Just tell him. You need to share it with him."

"Why?"

"You said you'd do anything for me. You agreed. I've Noor as my witness."

"Maia! No wonder Mohammed fell for your charm. You're impossible to say 'no' to. Okay. I'll tell him, if I must."

Maia smiled a very self-satisfied smile. "Good."

"Although there's no point. I won't be staying here."

"Just tell him. As soon as you get back to Sitra, tell him."

* * *

The soft beams of sunlight filtered through the fretwork of the ancient screen, casting intricate shadows on Razeen's desk. He closed his laptop and rubbed his eyes.

"Your next appointment is here, Your Majesty."

Razeen frowned. "I don't have one."

"The person showed up and I thought you'd want to see her."

"Her?"

His new assistant grinned and Razeen leaped up. It could only mean one thing. "Show her in."

Razeen waited for her to enter. He wanted to stride over and sweep her into his arms but he couldn't rush her. She'd kept a reserve with him, despite all that had happened. He gripped the back of the chair in an effort to stop himself. He failed.

He walked over and pulled her into his arms. "Lucy." He tipped her chin up so he could see the expression in her eyes. It wasn't reassuring. He let his hands slide back to his side and he showed her to a seat. He sat in his chair on the other side of his desk, hoping he'd be able to keep his distance. "How's Maia settled back into her home?"

Lucy huffed and shook her head. "I don't know how she could live like that." She shrugged. "But she seems happy and," she smiled, "Noor's thriving."

"Good." He couldn't take his eyes off her but she fixed her gaze on the desk, as if fascinated by the back of his computer.

"Well," she sighed, "I'm here to say goodbye."

Razeen's heart sank. "So soon?"

"May as well. Get back to my life."

His happiness at seeing her here evaporated instantly, replaced by irritation. How could she not see what was so patently obvious to him and to Maia. She belonged here with him. "And what life is that exactly?"

She looked at him with a sadness that immediately cut through his anger. "*My* life, that's what. Moving on, taking the next job and then the next."

"You can't go on forever like that."

She shrugged. "I don't see why not."

"Why not stop here, in Sitra? You love your sister, you'll see Noor grow up. I hear you haven't visited the clinic yet, despite numerous invitations. You could spend time with Aakifar and her family and friends."

Her face relaxed as she thought of her new friends. "Thanks for giving Aakifar such a great reference by the way. She loves her work at the clinic. They're great people and I hear the clinic is doing some really interesting work around diet and supplements. But—"

"Then, stay."

"They don't need me."

"Maybe, but I do."

She held his gaze. They were silent for long minutes. "*What*, are you talking about?"

"I want you to marry me, Lucy. I fell in love with you the moment I saw you, as you emerged from the sea, and it grows stronger all the time, whether you're here with me or not. I feel you here," he slammed his fist against his heart, "and I want you with me."

A sad smile spread over her face. "I've become acceptable, have I, with my interest in the clinic, with my rapport with the women? Is that it? Lucy Gee has suddenly become acceptable. Well, Razeen," she shook her head, "you're mistaken. I'm not acceptable, to me or to you."

"What the hell are you talking about, Lucy?"

"I have to tell you something." She looked down at her tightly clenched hands. "Something about me. It may help you understand." She shrugged. "Personally I don't think it will, but Maia has told me I have to tell you."

He frowned. "Go on."

"I have to keep moving, I simply have to. I don't stay in one place for long. I can't."

"I know, you've said that you're determined to experience everything, to enjoy life to its fullest. But I was hoping your recent experience might have changed things. That you may see that living here, staying in one place here, with me, could bring you happiness."

"You need a wife who will be happy staying in one place, a wife who wants children. I am not that wife and I never intend to have children."

"That will change."

"*No*, it won't."

"Lucy," he reached out and grabbed

her shaking hands. She slid them away from him.

"I was fifteen years old when I had a baby."

Pain sliced into his gut. So this was at the root of it. He swallowed dryly, dredging up the self-control he needed not to leap around the desk and take her in his arms. That wouldn't help her. Only talking would. "Go on."

"It was an easy birth." She didn't look up at him, just kept talking to the desk. "Not like Maia's." She half-laughed. "No, it was afterwards that things went from bad to worse. I didn't want to see the baby, rejected it outright. And, because of my age, the doctors, social workers and Maia, agreed to my demands to adopt the child out. It was only much later that I was diagnosed with postnatal depression." She still didn't look into his eyes, as if she was scared what she'd find there. "So, you see, I'm not fit to be a mother. Children, marriage, that's for other people, that's what people do who live life the right way. Not me. I don't know how to do anything other than hurt people and keep on moving." His eyes followed the agitated movements of her hands as she sank her fingernails hard into the palm of the other hand, as if to replace the pain she was feeling inside with physical pain. She cleared her throat. "Haven't you got anything to say?"

"What happened to the child?"

"He died. Young. A preventable ailment—dietary deficiency—I won't go into details but it turned out the people who adopted him had less of a clue how to bring up a child than I did. If I'd kept him with me he would have lived."

"Hence your interest here."

"Of course. I'm always trying to make up for it, always angry with myself. So now you know how stupid I am."

"Yes."

For the first time since she'd spoken

she looked at him with a sad, resigned smile. "You agree with me, then. I'm culpable."

"Yes, you're stupid. Yes, you're to blame. But not for what happened to you when you were little more than a child!" He leaped out of the chair and paced behind the desk. "You make me so angry. How could you punish yourself for such a thing? You were young and alone, apart from a sister who was also still a child. Of course you're not culpable. When will you stop punishing yourself?"

"Punishing myself? By moving around, having fun, enjoying new experiences?"

"Punishing yourself by running away. As soon as you might be happy, you're off. Stop it. Stay. Here. With me."

"Haven't you heard a word I've said?"

He continued to pace. "Do you remember when we first met? By the pool I explained about the *djullinar*, the monster who forces people to confront that which he or she dreads the most?"

"I remember. I think *you* are the *djullinar*. You've made me think more about my past than at any time over the past eight years."

"Then do something about it. *Lucy*, you were only fifteen. You can't go on blaming yourself forever. You're young, you have a life to lead, a life here, with me." He stopped pacing, grabbed her hands and held them tight, circling his thumbs over her tight fists. "What do I have to do to make you see?"

"You need a family. You need children. I can't go there. I can't risk it. I'm no good at that stuff."

"Really? And how exactly do you know this?"

"I just know."

He dropped her hands. "If you loved me you'd risk it. You obviously don't love me enough." He felt sick with anger, frustration and a love she didn't want.

She didn't move immediately. He could practically name the emotions as they flitted across her expressive face. Confusion, sadness, resignation...

"I have to go. I have to leave." Her voice was so small, tiny and soft as if a wisp of wind would blow it away.

He reached out and looped his finger under the compass that swung at her neck. "And where will your compass take you this time? Alex said there'll always be a job for you with him."

"You asked him, didn't you?"

"Of course. I want you to be safe. I want you to be cared for, if I can't do it." He dropped the compass. "You'd better leave, then."

He wasn't going to make it easy for her. Why should he? He stood and watched as she turned and left. She'd stop any moment now. Surely she'd stop and see that he spoke sense. Then she quietly opened the door and he held his breath, waiting for her to turn around. But then she was gone and the door was closed. For a brief moment frustration filled him and he wanted to go after her and drag her into his arms, make her stay. But, he knew it would be pointless. He *felt* she loved him but without her saying so, he couldn't be sure. It was fear that was preventing her from staying, he was sure. But you couldn't *force* someone to confront their fears—he knew that from experience. But perhaps force wasn't the only way. He picked up the phone.

* * *

The invitation to the clinic had been unexpected and unwanted—it interfered with her travel plans and it interfered with the self-discipline she needed to leave Razeen. She might have managed to refuse it, just as she had the previous invitations, if it hadn't been hand delivered by Aakifah, with

351

her little sister on her hip, bright-eyed and mischievous, now fully recovered from her anemia.

As Lucy watched Aakifah chat easily with the women at the clinic, she realized just how much Aakifah loved her work there, and how well she fitted into the clinic. It made Lucy feel good to realize that she'd actually done something worthwhile for her friend.

After the receptionist exchanged a few words with Aakifah, she turned to Lucy with a puzzled expression. "The director who invited you has been called into a meeting and has asked me to introduce you to the newest patient. But she would like to discuss something with you later, after your visit." Aakifah appeared uncertain. "If that's all right with you, Lucy?"

"Sure." Lucy thought it odd, but guessed the nature of the clinic's work would make it hard for the director to stick to a schedule.

Aakifah took her to one end of a long room where a very young woman sat holding a baby tightly to her body. While her arms gripped the child, her eyes seemed disconnected, huge, terrified.

They greeted each other formally and then Aakifah drew up a couple of chairs beside the woman.

"This is Hala. Her husband is—"

"She has a husband at her age?" Lucy interrupted. "She can't be more than, what? Seventeen?"

Aakifah shrugged. "It's not unusual in our culture. Her husband is overseas earning money and she's living with his family but they don't understand why she cries all the time."

Lucy's hesitation was only brief. "Tell her that I cried all the time." She sucked in a difficult breath. "When I had my baby."

Aakifah raised her eyebrows in surprise but didn't say anything other than translate Lucy's words.

The young woman turned her large, stunned eyes to Lucy and spoke rapidly.

"She wants to know if your husband's family helped you."

Lucy's mind flew back to the teenage boy whom she barely knew and whose family she had certainly never met. She'd wanted love and it turned out the boy had just wanted sex. He'd moved on to someone else by the time she'd realized she was pregnant.

"No. They didn't."

"She says that that is sad and wants to know who helped you with your birth if your family didn't."

"Tell her, I was in hospital. I was very young—younger than her—but I had my sister with me."

Aakifah opened her mouth to translate Hala's reply but shook her head instead, her eyes full of unspoken sympathy for Lucy.

Lucy placed her hand on Aakifah. "It's okay. Tell me what she says."

"She wants to know what color eyes your baby had. Were they green like yours?"

Lucy swallowed back the pain and closed her eyes as if in thought. "Umm, let me see." But she could only visualize her baby with eyes either closed in sleep, or scrunched up as he screamed. And he'd been crying hard when she'd seen him the last time. She'd just left him in the bassinet, screaming, and she'd walked away and hidden in a remote corner of the hospital. She hadn't been found for hours. She gasped in a raw breath. "They were blue."

"And now? She wants to know if they're still blue."

If the first question had pierced her, this one probed deep within the wound. "Yes, still blue." Sometimes a lie was better than the truth. Harder for her, but easier for the young woman.

"She wants to know whether you hated your baby."

Lucy swallowed hard. "I..." It was too hard. But the young woman's eyes continued to bore into her with a desperation she recognized. "Hate is one word for it. I was scared. I didn't want it. And I hated myself as much as the baby."

Aakifah translated, her brows knit in confusion, her innate courtesy refusing to allow her to question Lucy herself.

"She wants to know how long the hate lasted."

Lucy bit her lip. "Not long. Tell her she has to take each day as it comes, accept help, look after herself and she'll soon find she looks on the baby with love. And that love will only deepen." Lucy rose and curled her hand around the baby's rounded cheek before dropping her hand to the woman's arm. "And tell her she's not alone.

Many, many women suffer like her with these feelings after birth and she will recover."

Lucy watched relief fill the women's face.

Aakifah turned to Lucy. "She says she thought she was alone in these feelings." Lucy shook her head and the young woman smiled. "She says to thank you for your words."

"She's welcome." Lucy stood up. "I need to go now. There are things..." She shook her head helplessly. The truth was that she'd had to dig deep into the hurt she carried around with her and her own grief now tore at her heart, demanding attention. She had to go before she broke down. "I think I need some air."

They walked in silence for a few moments until they reached a door out into a leafy courtyard. Aakifah turned to Lucy. "Is it true? All that you said?"

"Sort of. I stopped hating the baby all

right, but it was too late for me. I never stopped hating myself."

"Then I think it's about time you stopped, isn't it?"

Was it? Thinking back to the young, terrified woman, she suddenly saw herself, sitting there, terrified and hurting. The girl wasn't guilty of anything except honesty, just as she hadn't been guilty of anything. Was it too late to start really living?

* * *

Lucy hesitated in the shadows and her heart went out to Razeen, who stood, unmoving, on the stone balcony. His hands were thrust in his pockets, weariness was evident in the tension of his shoulders, as he gazed blankly out to the violet sky, where the white vapor trail of the plane Lucy should have been on could still be seen.

"Razeen..." Perhaps she spoke too softly because while Razeen stiffened a little, he didn't move, merely shook his head as if to clear it of some thought.

She stepped toward him but before she could touch him he turned and she stopped dead in her tracks, arrested by the intensity of his expression. He opened his mouth to speak but nothing emerged. He cleared his throat.

"You didn't leave then."

She shook her head and smiled, feeling suddenly uncertain. "No."

"Did you miss your flight? Going tomorrow instead?"

She shook her head again. "No. Well, I don't know. I thought that I might, well, stay." He was silent and she continued, trying to fill the silence with words, any words, anything that might dilute the tension in the air. "I, er, went to the clinic. It was," she shrugged, blinking, "amazing. They offered me work there. And I thought that I might..." she made the mistake of catching his hot gaze, "stay..."

"Stay…" His lips quirked but his eyes were still sad. "You'd stay for the job. That's good. I'm pleased. I'm sure you'll enjoy it."

"Yes," she nodded, wanting to elaborate, wanting to tell him exactly what happened to her in the clinic, but unable to find the words under his intense gaze. "I, umm…"

"How long will you stay?"

A direct question she could deal with. "I have no plans to move on."

He took a step toward her. "No plans? What happened to the woman who had to keep moving, keep on running. Where did she go?"

"She stopped running. She found a man who believed in her, made her want to stay."

He closed his eyes as if in pain and dropped his forehead to hers. "I thought you'd gone. I thought you'd left me."

"No, I'm here. And, if you want me,

I'll stay here. I love you, Razeen." He picked up her compass and examined it as if trying to buy himself time. For one long moment she wondered if she'd got it wrong, if he didn't love her after all. But she had to continue; she had to find out. "Razeen, don't you understand, the compass is pointing to you."

"I understand completely. It means, Lucy, you can always find me."

"Only if you want to be found."

He smiled and slipped his fingers through her hair and brought her face up to his. His breath was warm on her face, the curl of his lips inviting; but it was in his eyes that she finally found the answer she'd been looking for, the answer confirmed by the whispered word pressed against her lips. "Always."

EPILOGUE

Lucy waded through the shallows and onto the still warm sand. It was early evening—her favorite time of day. The violet haze that held the darkness in check would be gone momentarily and the remote Lodge would be a sole beacon of light in the surrounding darkness. She always enjoyed her solitary swim but only because she knew what awaited her.

She ran up the short flight of steps onto the wooden verandah, plucked a towel from a pile and quickly dried herself.

Silently she walked along the dark wooden floorboards and pushed open a door. The twins were fast asleep, the night light showing Taban lying on his front, covers thrown off, his pyjama-clad bottom sticking up in the air, his head covered by a much-loved brontosaurus. She smiled to herself. She imagined Razeen was like their son as a child. On the go from morning until night when he fell asleep in whatever position he was last in. She gently eased him down into the bed, uncovered his head and tucked him in, laying a soft kiss on his cheek. He muttered something incomprehensible and fell straight back to sleep.

Then Lucy turned to Sabuhi. She lay on her side, both hands tidily tucked under her cheek. She was as dark-skinned as her twin was fair; as serious, as her brother was light-hearted. She stroked the thick, luscious hair, tucked a hot strand away from her face and lowered a kiss to her cheek. Sabuhi's eyes flickered open, she smiled trustingly and reached for Lucy's hand and brought it to her lips. "Love you, Ommy."

Lucy brought the joint fists to her own lips, in a nightly routine that always seemed to settle her more highly-strung daughter. "Love you more. Sleep tight, baby."

She turned at the door and gazed upon her two children, overwhelmed with thankfulness. She jumped as Razeen pulled her hard against his body and slipped his hands around her pregnant stomach in a sweet caress. "So, not twins this time."

"No, just the one. Shame."

"Why?"

She pulled the door closed, turned to him and kissed him deeply. "It'll take us longer to reach the required number."

"And that is?"

"At least one more than Maia. We're very competitive, you know." She couldn't help grinning at his expression. "And she wants at least four."

"Four? But that means—"

"Six, at least six. Can't have an odd number."

"And you know what that also means?"

She shook her head.

"Practice. Lots of practice."

He slipped his hands to her bottom and he drew her tight against his hips and kissed her in a way that made her forget about numbers, about everything except the power of the love that existed between them: a power greater than any magnetic force on earth.

THE END

Dear Reader,

Thank you for reading *The Sheikh's Lost Lover*. I hope you enjoyed it! Reviews are always welcome—they help me, and they help prospective readers to decide if they'd enjoy the book.

This is the third book in the Desert Kings series which comprises:

Wanted: A Wife for the Sheikh
The Sheikh's Bargain Bride
The Sheikh's Lost Lover
Awakened by the Sheikh
Claimed by the Sheikh
Wanted: A Baby by the Sheikh

The fourth book—*Awakened by the Sheikh*—features Tariq and Cara (excerpt follows). Here's a review of Awakened by the Sheikh to give you a taste of what to expect.

"This book and series has everything. Love romance sensuality mystery and intrigue…" (Amazon.com)

For more information about my books and to sign up to my newsletter, please check out my website: www.dianafraser.com.

Happy reading!

Diana

***

Awakened by the Sheikh

Book 4 of Desert Kings—Tariq

Cara Devlin's sexy voice lands her the job as translator to the King of Ma'in with a salary that will ensure she can leave Ma'in, and the painful memories of a husband who used her, and start afresh. King Tariq is devoted to his children, his country and remaining single. He soon realizes Cara could prove useful in his business negotiations... but only providing she doesn't know she's being used.

Excerpt

"You're silent, Cara. I have been killing time, swimming, trying to get you out of my mind. Waiting until breakfast when I could reasonably see you again."

She swallowed, hardly daring to believe what she was hearing.

"Are you feeling the same as me?"

He brushed aside her hair. "Tell me now, if you are not, and I will take my hand from your arm. Tell me quickly," he whispered as he dipped his head to hers, "so that I make no mistakes."

She sucked in a sudden breath, as his closeness deluged her senses with his smell, his presence, his eyes, his lips, so close to hers. But she didn't want to make a mistake either. "I don't know what you're feeling so how can I say if it's the same?"

He lifted a strand of her hair, his eyes tracing the twist of it between his fingertips. "So cautious. Well, I shan't be. Each hour of each day I've been with you, you've revealed yourself to me, little by little, as if your brightness would be too overwhelming to be revealed all at once. I've never known such hunger to be with someone. The more I know about you, the more I want to know. I think about you at night, before I sleep, and I think about you once more when I awake. And then there are my dreams. Cara, I want to make love to you, but only if you are sure, because I cannot promise anything beyond now. My relationships are, by necessity, brief and casual. I want my children to be raised correctly, with no whisper of scandal. There can be no future for us... only now."

She nodded, her throat too constricted to say anything. Her breath hitched in her lungs and her eyes watered with emotion. He frowned as if not sure of her meaning. She nodded again more vigorously. "Yes," she managed to whisper. "Yes, I want you. And just for now works for me, too."

She could have it all. Him. Now. And then, tell him the truth later when he no longer wanted her.

He took her hand and they retraced their steps back to the palace. Except, this time, they made their way to Tariq's suite.

BOOKLIST

—The Mackenzies—

The Real Thing
The PA's Revenge
The Marriage Trap
The Cowboy's Craving
The Playboy's Redemption
The Lakehouse Café

—New Zealand Brides—

Yours to Give
Yours to Treasure
Yours to Cherish

—Desert Kings—

Wanted: A Wife for the Sheikh
The Sheikh's Bargain Bride
The Sheikh's Lost Lover
Awakened by the Sheikh
Claimed by the Sheikh
Wanted: A Baby by the Sheikh

—Italian Romance—

Perfect
Her Retreat
Trusting Him
An Accidental Christmas

ABOUT THE AUTHOR

Diana lives with her family in a small seaside community north of Wellington, New Zealand, with two cocker spaniels who bark at everything and a tortoise-shell cat who teases them mercilessly.

She writes contemporary romantic fiction and has four series on the go: Desert Kings (sheikh romances), Italian Romance, and the Mackenzies and New Zealand Brides series, both of which are set in New Zealand. She has more books planned in each series and if you'd like an email letting you know when new books are published, you can subscribe to Diana's newsletter via her website: wwww.dianafraser.net.